PROMISES
TO
KEEP

A Story Of Destiny

A Novel by

Nicki Charest

ISBN- 978-0-578-53801-3

Promises To Keep

Proudly self-published through Divine Legacy Publishing, www.divinelegacypublishing.com
Cover Design: Terrika Foster-Brasby
1st Editor: Amanda Chambers, www.theeditingchambers.com
2nd Editor: Ashley Campbell

Acknowledgments

My second novel... SHUT THE F* UP! I promise I told my editor Amanda Chamber I was only writing one book. She didn't believe me, but she believed IN me and for that I will always be grateful. Amanda you push me to be better and I honestly don't know where I would be without you. Thank you. I love you Sis!!!

My readers and followers, ya'll are the bomb! Ya'll really make me feel like I know what I'm doing (LOL). But seriously, thank you for your continuous support. I come damn near to tears when I think about how much you all uplift me.

My husband Greg, I did it again babe. Thanks for giving me silence when I need it so I can write!

My Divine Legacy Publishing Family, I absolutely adore you all. You keep pushing me to be great and to keep up with ya'll lol... Author Jennifer Robinson, Author Michelle Warren, K. Fitz (my bro!), Brandon Walker (my other bro), Asia, Author Daneal Brown, all ya'll! I really thank God for you all!

My Sisters, my backbones. Ya'll know who ya'll are. When I lost those 10 chapters and thought I was going to die... thanks for the motivation lol (ORDA = LOVE)

My Sorors of Sigma Gamma Rho Sorority, Inc. Your support means everything and I appreciate all of you who continuously take this journey with me. Special shout out to my home chapter Theta Alpha Sigma (#OneTAS #OneSIGMA)

My family: I'm still working on that goal of making you all proud to say you're related to me. Whether you are with me by birth or by marriage, you're stuck with me. ☺

Thank you everyone... I mean it 1,000 times over!

1

Ladies Man

"Fuck. Fuck! FUCK!"

Monica's screams of pleasure and pain resonated all the way through Monarch Apartments. She was engaged in a dance between bodies that felt to be never ending. For two straight hours, nothing but her voice and the sound of the bed rails lightly tapping against the walls could be heard. It wasn't uncommon to hear the sound of sex coming from Derrick Goodwin's apartment. Though the voices might change from weekend to weekend, the loud moaning from apartment 1108 was the norm.

See, Derrick was something like a player. He enjoyed entertaining several women at once and didn't like the idea of settling down. To him, it was a waste of time. After growing up in a household with a father who often forgot he was a married man, Derrick didn't want the stress of being tied down to one person. He remembered the hurt on his mother's face every time she found out about another woman that his father had added to his long list of infidelities. Derrick knew his father was a serial cheater and had even occasionally accompanied his dad on some of his unfaithful escapades.

As a kid, Derrick really didn't think much of it. In fact, he thought it was rather adventurous to be around his father while he went to "have a drink with friends." But as Derrick matured, it didn't take him long to discover how those friendly visits were unbeknownst to his mother. Seeing her cry upset him, and seeing his father continue to lie to her about it with weak, insincere apologies angered him further. It was in those moments that Derrick decided he didn't want to see that look on any of the women's faces that he'd date, nor did he ever want to lie to them about his intentions. He would not be his father. And he carried that mantra well into his adult years. He found it was usually best to be very upfront with women about not being exclusive. But if there was one female he'd consider wifing, it would be the one he was currently laying pipe to: Monica Lawrence. Monica was no ordinary girl to Derrick; she was different.

Derrick and Monica had known each other since they were freshman in high school. She was from Hartford, but through the use of a relative's address, she managed to attend West Hartford High. Monica was one tough cookie back then. She was always top of the class, always no nonsense, and always ready to debate if she felt she was right – which most of the time she was - so it was no surprise to Derrick when several years later he ran into her at a café in Palo Alto while attending Stanford Law School. Turns out, Monica was a student there as well.

It was gratifying for Derrick to see a familiar face among the many he'd encountered at Stanford. Their friendship was rekindled, and they became true support systems for each other through the difficult curriculum that was Stanford Law. The two ended up taking a couple of classes together, studying for the bar together, and even considered opening a practice together back home in Hartford. But over time, their relationship took a different direction - a physical one.

Derrick always had a thing for Monica, even back in high school before her 5 foot 6 inch frame had 36 DDD breasts to accompany it. He loved the flawlessness of her mocha skin, the curve of her waist, and the enchanting smile she possessed. But most of all, he admired how she stayed true to her Afrocentric lifestyle, even after growing into a professional attorney in a mainstream corporate world.

Back when they were legal interns, Monica often wore her hair in braided Mohawks or rocked kinky twists that showed off her natural hair's thickness. She accessorized her wardrobe with ankh necklaces, Africa shaped earrings, and kente cloth type headbands. Her loungewear consisted of "Fight the Power" and "Black Girl Magic" tshirts, and her favorite color was purple, which she described as a tribute to her African royal lineage. Monica was so unapologetically black, and Derrick was captivated by her love of self and love of culture.

Derrick could still remember the first time he acted upon his desires for her. After a long night of studying for the bar in the Munger graduate dorms, Monica was making coffee, as they were both pretty tired. Derrick couldn't help but notice the way her yoga pants hugged her size 8 hips. He often thought to himself that Monica's ass was a balloon waiting to be popped; those yoga pants made him anxious to burst it. He became aroused and was nervous about making his next move, but as soon as she handed him his cup of coffee, Derrick decided it was now or never. He placed his cup on the small table next to where Monica was sitting, purposely angling himself over her. He glanced in her eyes and without warning, planted a sweet and soft kiss right on her lips. It caught her off guard, but to Derrick's surprise, and delight, she embraced it.

"We're not supposed to be doing this," Monica warned after finally pulling her lips away from Derrick.

"I know . . . yet something else in me is saying this is exactly what we're supposed to be doing," Derrick replied.

With his right hand on her cheek and his left hand on her thigh, he continued to kiss her deeply, eventually laying her body flat on the couch. It was almost impossible to stop the flame that was burning inside them both that night.

4

The entire time, Derrick couldn't help but think that Monica would want to stop and would shoo off his advances. He didn't want to ruin their friendship, no matter how attracted he was to her. He respected her more than any woman he had ever met and didn't want things to become awkward between them. He valued her friendship more than anything because he'd never felt about anyone the way he felt about her. But that night in Munger, he wanted more. He needed more. He got more. And he has been getting more ever since.

Monica was no dummy. She knew that Derrick wasn't a "one woman's man" type of guy. They were clear to each other that they were not exclusive. Plus, she'd been friends with this man long enough to see the various women he kept in and out of his bed.

When their relationship dynamic changed, her mindset about Derrick didn't at first. She still saw him as a close friend and she never led herself to believe that any kind of relationship other than the friendship they shared could happen between them. She enjoyed the sex and the company. But inevitably, feelings begin to develop and Monica was finding it more and more complicated to stay in the friend zone when she saw Derrick with other women.

After knowing him for 13 years and sleeping with him for the last three, what they were doing just wasn't cutting it for her anymore. They were no longer Stanford students finding comfort in each other. She was ready for something more concrete in her life. And while she didn't wanted to stop being friends with Derrick, Monica needed to free herself of him as her lover.

She had only come over to his place to let him know that whatever this fling was that they called themselves having was over. At least that was her intention when she'd entered Derrick's apartment just moments before she was screaming his name.

The second she walked in and Derrick saw her in that army green cat suit and those tan 4-inch sandals, every word she spoke went in one ear and out the other. Her outfit accentuated every curve of her body. Her perfectly manicured nails matched the polish of her toes that were shown from the peep of her shoes, and Derrick had a fetish for pretty feet. In that moment, Derrick thought she was the sexiest woman he had ever seen and refused to let her finish "breaking it off."

He grabbed her by the arm and swung her body against the wall before passionately kissing her to hush her. Monica attempted to pull away, wanting to really break things off with Derrick, but it was too late. She was caught in his trance once again and began to feel her body tense from Derrick's touches. Her emotional attachment kicked in and she yielded to her yearning for him.

Derrick picked her up and carried her upstairs to the bedroom where he slowly removed her one-piece, exposing her breasts that he loved so much. He softly kissed the top of them, not yet removing them from her bra, and used his fingertips to gently rub her clit through her panties. Monica was dripping with moisture and

Derrick was so erect from the aura of her that he couldn't even continue the foreplay. He needed to take her right then, right at that moment.

Hour after hour, he fucked Monica until she was weak. She had cum so much that neither of them could keep track of the number. Derrick wanted to make sure she would think twice before coming to break off what they had again. Although she wasn't his girl officially, he selfishly didn't want to lose her or see her with someone else.

As she approached her final climax, he stroked her faster and faster, affirming that she was not going anywhere anytime soon:

"You leaving me baby?" Derrick asked with each stroke. "Huh? You leaving me?"

"Oh God," Monica moaned. "No. No."

"I didn't think so. This is me. Every part of you is mine. Right?"

"Yes baby, it's yours," she replied.

Derrick's authoritative tone took ownership of Monica's body and mind, but it was only for a split second. Squeezing Derrick tightly, Monica climaxed loudly, screaming to the top of her lungs the kinds of oohs you would find in a Jenna Jameson video.

Weak and exhausted, Monica lay comfortably aside Derrick. She began to think maybe, just maybe, Derrick was coming around and would finally decide to settle down. *Maybe I was too hasty in wanting to end this*, she thought to herself. But reality hit almost instantaneously, for as soon as the comfort sank in, Derrick's phone began to vibrate. It was a text message and Monica didn't need to see from whom. She glanced over at the clock to see it was a little past 11:15pm. She figured whoever it was had a vagina that Derrick would soon be entering and that text made it all more clear that she should have followed her first mind instead of getting suckered into his bed again. But, while her head was telling her not to be stupid, her heart was saying the complete opposite.

Monica just needed to be honest with Derrick. She needed to tell him that she wanted more. She desperately wanted him to know that she was in love with him, that she knew he was in love with her too, and that he could let down his guard and give himself to her. He didn't need these other women, he only thought he did.

She was ready to say that to him in hopes he would agree and they could make love until the morning sun. But before she could formulate the first word of the sentence, Derrick had already rolled over and begun to look for his wife beater and jogging pants.

What Monica didn't know was that Derrick already had plans for the night and didn't expect Monica to be at his place. While he didn't want to seem like a jerk, he definitely wanted to follow through on the arrangements he'd previously made. Without a second thought, Derrick went to the bathroom to freshen up and prepared to be on his way to answer the text.

Monica knew all the shit Derrick spoke when fucking her was just for the moment and not to be taken seriously; she had accepted that a long time ago. But he'd never been so out of his mind to literally get out of the bed with her to go fuck with someone else. That was a breaking point. Monica was annoyed, felt highly disrespected, and most of all she was hurt.

Derrick had often left Monica at his place while he was gone for various reasons, so he didn't mind her being there while he was out. But he was completely ignorant to her current fury. When he grabbed his keys and began to head towards to the door, Monica smacked her lips loudly sitting up against the headboard with a look of disgust on her face.

Knowing he needed to properly say goodbye to her, he walked over to where she was sitting on the bed. He approached her with a grin on his face, reaching in to kiss her lips, but Monica swiftly and harshly turned her face. She looked in Derrick's eyes and with confusion in her voice asked, "Why do you fuck me like you love me?"

"Huh?" Derrick said abruptly. He was taken aback by Monica's question and took a few steps away from the bed, even dropping his head a bit in shame. He opened his mouth to answer her, but no words could leave his lips.

There was nothing he could muster that could properly convey his feelings for her, nor accurately explain why they could never be. He didn't want to lie to her. He DID love her, but not in the way that she needed him to. Derrick didn't trust himself with Monica. He knew he would screw it up. As much as being a chip off the old block was not an option, in the end he feared he would turn out exactly like his father. He didn't want to do what his father did to his mother to anyone, least of all to

Monica. So committing to her and only her was not in the cards. He thought Monica understood that, but Derrick looked at her and knew in that moment he may have just broken her heart.

Maybe she was right, maybe we do need to break this off, Derrick said to himself as he gazed at Monica and thought she was so beautiful and how happy she would make some guy some day. He slowly kissed her on the forehead and backed away from the bed. He turned towards the door, quietly making his way to the door.

Monica sat on the bed in disbelief, fighting the tears she knew she shouldn't shed.

Hearing her cry only affirmed to Derrick that he was becoming more like his father everyday. Opening the door Derrick finally answered her question: "Because I do love you Monica... but sometimes love ain't enough."

With those words, he closed the door behind him and stood there in the hallway. He could hear Monica's sobs through the door. He couldn't front; it ate at him. He wanted to open that door and tell her what she wanted to hear if it would turn the water works off. But he would also be lying to her. He'd never done that to Monica in 13 years. He wasn't about to start now. So he walked away.

When Derrick reached the elevator, he looked at his phone to respond to the text: I'm on the way.

Stepping onto the elevator, he looked back at his apartment and thought for a quick second to go back in there. He decided against it.

He shook his head and mumbled to himself, "Chip off the old block." As the doors closed before him, he looked at his phone and pressed send.

Promises To Keep

2
The Office Grind

"You've reached the office of Derrick Goodwin. Please hold."

"No calls right now Bernice," Derrick said while waving his hands no, but it was too late. The phone in his office was already ringing, as his secretary Bernice had patched the caller through.

Dammit, he thought to himself. When he walked past Bernice's desk, he turned back to look at her with a sarcastic smirk. "Never mind. I guess I'm taking it. "

Derrick hadn't been in the building for more than five minutes. He wasn't prepared to speak with any clients just yet, and he hadn't had his morning coffee. He hadn't had a chance to review any emails or check his daily schedule.

Hell, he hadn't even fully taken his jacket off. But what was really weighing on him was that he hadn't cleared his mind from Saturday night with Monica.

He hadn't spoken to her since that night. In fact, he felt so bad about how he had left things with her that he left his appointment with Sonya after being there for only a few mins. As he had expected, Monica wasn't at his place when he returned.

Derrick cared for Monica more than he wanted to admit and it bothered him that he had not yet had a chance to reconcile with her. He just needed a few minutes to get it together and clear his mind before starting the day, yet thanks to Bernice the workday for Derrick Goodwin Esq. had officially begun.

Despite this miscommunication, Bernice was a great assistant; the best Derrick had since he'd been with the firm. She was very organized and detailed, and she always looked stunning. Her perfume was so unique and so distinctive that when you smelled a soft tropical fragrance, you knew it was Bernice. It was like coconut oil and pineapples met and made a baby. He could only be mad at Bernice for so long because she literally lit up the room with her scent and her smile. It wasn't uncommon for other attorneys in the firm to compliment Derrick on his luck in gaining Bernice as an assistant. Derrick had even thought to himself a time or two that if he had met Bernice at any other place in any other time, she would surely be on his weekly list of things to do.

Derrick was an attorney at McEnroe & Associates, or MEA, one of the most prestigious law firms in New England. He began his career there shortly after graduating from Stanford. At 28 years old, Derrick was already one of the most sought out attorneys in the New England area, largely due to his role in the Cedrick St. James case he'd won just 18 months prior at the mere age of 27. It was a case that would change his life.

Cedrick St. James was accused of the first-degree murder of 67 year-old Vernon Tout. St. James was an upstanding citizen and businessman in the Greater Hartford area. Tout had previously refused to sell his land to St. James, who wanted to build residences on it. St. James' company, Right Time Realty, provided homes to many of the city's most impoverished residents at little to no cost. He was heavily into giving back to the community in various ways and St. James saw use for the property other than storing old cars, tires, and an assortment of other scrap that Tout kept there creating much of a junkyard with the land.

Somewhere in negotiations for the property there was a disconnection between Tout and St. James. They continuously fought about the property until the spout became public. Tout made a statement that St. James would get that property "over his dead body." Three days later, Tout's body was found in the Connecticut River.

McEnroe & Associates represented some of New England's most prominent businessmen and elite figures. Right Time Realty, while elite in stature, was not financially in the tax bracket of most MEA clients, but managed to be represented by them under American Bar Association Model Rule 6.1, which states a lawyer should aspire to commit at least 50 hours of pro bono legal services a year. Because St. James was wealthy enough to afford legal counsel, but not quite at the level of affording MEA, the firm believed this case was perfect to fulfill their requirement to the ABA.

Derrick always felt his selection to represent St. James was not on his ability to provide a solid defense, but more so about his racial similarity to the defendant. Currently there were only four African-American associates in the entire firm, and none of which were employed by MEA at the time the case was being heard. Derrick also felt this was simply a ploy for the firm to claim they were advocates for diversity, even though internally they couldn't care less if St. James fried or not for the crime. So, St. James paid a cheaper than usual fee to retain MEA for his defense. However, what the partners didn't anticipate was how big of a story the case would eventually turn out to be.

Publicly it became another case of a black man being wrongfully accused of murdering a white victim. This was a criminal justice gold mine - and Derrick was holding the axe to crack it open.

The local NAACP got involved in the case and opted to pay for St. James' legal defense. They backed Derrick one hundred percent and the case began to garner national attention. Considering the evidence against him, the prosecution framed a character assassination against St. James, sparking quite a controversy.

They targeted his upbringing in Brooklyn, NY, his prior criminal history, and the fact that he was the last person that many key witnesses said Tout was seen with.

Derrick worked diligently to discredit several of the prosecution's key witnesses. He was able to get some of the evidence thrown out on technicalities, but more importantly, he was able to prove his client's innocence. St. James' alibi wasn't the tightest, but that, along with DNA evidence, was enough to prove that St. James was not the culprit. The real killer had yet to be found. In turn, Derrick gained national notoriety and a hefty payday that allowed him to live a lavish lifestyle.

Most partners in the firm were thoroughly impressed by Derrick: how he handled the media attention, his jury selection, and his overall presentation to the case was stellar. He made good on his Stanford education and after the case, he became a household name across the state and the northeast.

Immediately after, Derrick was promoted to senior associate and earned himself a corner office with his name on the door, a personal assistant, a reserved parking space, and a billboard on the side of I-84. He knew it was only a matter of time before he'd make partner and most other partners believed so as well. All except for the CEO of MEA, Rich McEnroe III.

Rich was the elder of the McEnroe brothers who ran the company. He and his brother Christopher McEnroe inherited the firm from their father, the late Rich McEnroe

Jr., and were the only two equity partners in the two-tier structure of the firm. Sure, non-equity partners made money, but Rich and Chris made the money and the decisions, and Rich wasn't afraid to remind anyone who was the boss. Between the two brothers, it was usually Rich that carried the final say. It was also Rich that most people who worked with MEA despised the most.

He had an entitlement problem. He felt like he owed nothing, but he carried himself as if he had earned everything. He belittled his employees, spoke to people condescendingly, and was quite frequently racially insensitive. Among other things, Rich was by far the least knowledgeable in the field of law. He lost more cases than he'd won, and didn't score anywhere near what Derrick had on the BAR exam. Internally, Rich knew he didn't measure up to Derrick and this fueled a jealousy that grew to new heights after Derrick's success with the firm.

Rich wasn't too thrilled with the attention Derrick received after the St. James case. To be frank, he hated it. He loathed the many clients who called MEA were looking to be represented specifically by Derrick, and he loathed even more the mere thought that Derrick could ever sit at the table with him and the other partners. No African-American had ever been offered a seat at the MEA table, and Rich had no plans on making history. It was an unspoken rule known to many that he was not going to make a black man senior partner of McEnroe & Associates, including Derrick.

Rich decided enough was enough with the Derrick Goodwin popularity contest and began to have assistants reroute referrals for Derrick to other associates in the firm. After a few weeks, Derrick noticed his voicemail inbox was continuously filled with potential clients, yet his client list was becoming smaller and smaller. He was quick to realize that him being a heavy favorite to make partner made Rich saltier than a bag of Lays.

It was a good strategy on the part of Rich. Rerouting clients made Derrick's push for partner a bit harder - you can't win cases you aren't given. It crossed his mind on many occasions to start his own practice and he previously brought the topic up to Monica, who undoubtedly would have been his partner. But she had her own successes unfolding in the firm she worked for and was riding the wave a little longer before considering stepping out. Besides, Derrick couldn't leave MEA anyway, no matter how bad he wanted to and he had himself to thank for that.

As fine of a lawyer as he was, Derrick carried personal baggage. Rarely did it ever interfere with his professional life, but the one instance it did, it landed Derrick in front of the courts with his license on the line facing disbarment.

Rich's brother Chris vouched for his ethics and the punishment was reduced from disbarment to a suspension. Derrick tried not to think about how his womanizing ways had almost cost him his career, but he was consistently reminded of his shortcoming every time he thought about leaving. Until his probation period was over, he had to remain under the supervision of Chris, which ultimately meant he had to remain at MEA and continue working for Rich. He was thankful that the situation never became public and didn't interfere with his ability to try the St. James case, but he never stopped counting down the days when the suspension would be over. The quicker it came, the quicker he could wash his hands of Rich.

***

The day was getting away from him. It was already fifteen minutes to one and Derrick had yet to grab lunch, so he decided to order out. He still had a few cases to scramble through and a few follow up calls to make. Time was money to Derrick, and he didn't want to lose any more time. He messaged his secretary who was hard at work doing nothing; however, the moment she saw a message from Derrick pop up on her screen, she immediately put down her nail file to give him her attention. She turned in her chair to see Derrick's grin and elected to return his message with a phone call to his desk instead.

"Yes, Mr. Goodwin?"

"Hey Bernice, can you place an order for that Cajun Chicken and Shrimp lunch platter I like?"

"That kind of day, huh Mr. Goodwin?" Bernice questioned. She knew him well enough to know if he was eating fried foods for lunch, he was stressed.

Derrick wasn't a health nut, but he was mindful of his diet and didn't eat too heavy during the middle of the day. He only asked for fried chicken and shrimp for lunch when he was bothered by a case or had a lot on his mind. For him, it was the best substitute for a shot of Crown Royal.

"You have no idea, Bernice. Been that kind of week actually," Derrick answered.

"It's just Monday Mr. Goodwin. Your week hasn't even started yet," Bernice chuckled.

"Which further proves why I need this Cajun Chicken and Shrimp," Derrick laughed.

Bernice shook her head simpering and assured Derrick she would get his platter before hanging up the call. In fact, she would have given him whatever he wanted and not just food. While she did enjoy working for him and considered him to be a thoughtful, kind, and caring boss, she also acknowledged he was sexy as sin.

Bernice had been crushing on Derrick since she started working there a year ago. As assistants talk, she heard about the reputation he had with the ladies, but she didn't care; it intrigued her more. She had every intention on finding out if the gossips were true on her own. The tingle Bernice felt in between her thighs each time she entered the office of the 6'0" dark skinned specimen she called her boss was getting closer and closer to being unbearable. She often subliminally flirted with Derrick and tried to make herself available to him at every minute of the day. She'd previously invited Derrick out a time or two to hang with her and some of the other associates in the office, but he was always either "too busy" or "not available." Bernice always maintained her professionalism, never truly letting on to her internal yearning to taste the sweetness of his chocolate, but she felt she was going to have to take drastic measures in order for him to get the hint.

As 2:00 approached, Derrick received an email from Bernice:

"Mr. Goodwin,

Your order has arrived and is waiting for you in the break room in the north wing. The south wing break room was filled and I know you would prefer to not be bothered. Considering no one ever goes there, I felt that was more appropriate for your mood. As a treat to lift your spirits, I ordered you a dessert on me. – B"

Aw, Bernice is such a doll, Derrick thought to himself. He was starving and appreciated Bernice's thoughtfulness.

While he waited for the food, he'd sent an email to Monica and had not yet heard a reply. He would have preferred to eat in his office so he didn't miss her email in case she responded, but then again, maybe he needed to step away for a second to regroup. Derrick grabbed his cell, closed and coded his door, and headed towards the north wing break room. He wanted to thank Bernice for her kindness, but realized she hadn't returned to her desk yet. No surprise to Derrick, he was sure she was on lunch as well.

The north wing of the building was under renovation, so everyone had been moved from that area. It was mostly closed off, but due to contract negotiations being at a stalemate with the architect designing the new wing, the construction had been temporarily halted. Only a select few were aware that the break room, restroom, and exit doors were still accessible on that end. Whenever Derrick wanted a moment of peace, he'd have Bernice set an away message and he'd escape to the north wing.

When he entered the break room, he grinned at Bernice's efforts. She had his food portioned on a plate, silverware placed on the table, bottled water, napkins, and a copy of The Hartford Courant ready for him to skim while he ate.

"Bernice is the best I swear," Derrick mumbled to himself cheesing from ear to ear and thankful that he had the kind of assistant who would go to such lengths for him.

He sat down ready to dig into his platter when suddenly he heard a voice calling his name. Derrick looked around the small and empty break room and saw nothing.

"Damn I must really need a break," Derrick said aloud while continuing to eat. But not 30 seconds later, he once again heard what sounded like a whisper of his name.

He was pretty sure that he was alone on the wing, but just to cure his curiosity, he stood up and walked towards the kitchen area that was adjacent to the break room just to peep inside. The kitchen area was much bigger than the break room but it was part of the area of the wing where the construction had begun, which meant no one with any sense would actually be in there.

The two rooms were separated by a sliding door, which to Derrick's surprise appeared to be cracked open. It was dark, and Derrick could feel the chill of the darkness, as if the air had been turned on and was seeping from the door's threshold. He was skeptical about going inside. While the wing still had some electrical connections, this part of the kitchen area didn't have lighting. Derrick took one step past the threshold of the door and quickly changed his mind.

"Fuck this," Derrick decided. He turned around to head back in to the break room to finish his lunch, thinking he must have been nuts to really take his ass in that dark room. He wasn't the guy to just be creeping around in the dark in strange rooms for the sake of being nosey. But at that moment, he heard his name again and this time it was clear as day. Someone was in there.

"Yo, who's in here?" Derrick asked, sliding the door all the way open. He could see the shadow of someone as his eyes began adjusting to the darkness. "So I guess you're not going to answer me," Derrick asked in an annoyed tone while continuing to walk towards the figure.

As he got closer, Derrick began to pick up on a familiar scent. It was a fragrance he smelled around the office regularly and was one of his favorites. He knew exactly who was lurking in the dark and instantly became concerned. With the wing being under renovation, he was unsure if she was hurt and unable to speak above a whisper. However, as he approached her, he felt her leg stretch out and her shoeless foot, graze slightly against his zipper.

It caught him off guard. Gasping he spoke, "Bernice… what are you doing?"

But, she refused to speak. Derrick's concern turned into confusion. He could hear her moaning. With his eyes fully adjusted to the darkness, he could make out the shadow of her face and arms. She was biting her bottom lip and her arm was dropped to the side, rhythmically motioning to the sounds that were faintly coming from her mouth. She was pleasuring herself to the presence of Derrick.

Using her foot, she gestured for Derrick to come closer. With her blouse open and skirt raised, she grabbed Derrick by his shirt with both hands, pulling him close in between her thighs. Derrick wasn't expecting this behavior from Bernice, but he couldn't deny that her aggressive nature was turning him on. He'd not been oblivious to Bernice's previous advances, but for the sake of professionalism he tried his best to avoid the exact situation he currently found himself in. He didn't want anyone to claim any lawsuits against him for improper conduct in the workplace, but what was he to do at this point.

Bernice was a beautiful woman. Her milk chocolate skin and raspy voice often reminded him of the singer Brandy. He was a sucker for that coconut scent, which was Bernice's fragrance of choice, and his nose was fully fixed in it. Exposing her C cup breasts in the black sheer bra she was wearing, he was slowly losing his ability to contain himself. Her legs were as smooth and shiny as freshly polished brass, as he rubbed his hands along them. Derrick knew he shouldn't do this, but he was having a hard time convincing his body to agree with his mind.

"Bernice. I don't think this is appro-," but before he could finish, Bernice placed her fingers over his lips.

"Shhh," she whispered. "Dessert was on me, remember?"

She smirked at Derrick before biting her lower lip once again, which was becoming impossible for Derrick to ignore. Her lips were full and glossy from the MAC lip color she was wearing. Derrick was so entranced at how her mouth moved that he almost reached in to bite her bottom lip too. They glanced at each other for a split second before reaching in to engage in an intense kiss. Derrick's pants could no longer shield his growing erection and Bernice could feel his manhood rise. She began ripping his pants open, never unlocking her lips with his, until she was able to touch what she'd been yearning for.

Derrick unbuttoned the rest of her blouse and savagely began kissing on the top of her breast. The more she moaned at his kisses and touches, the less he remembered this was his secretary. He lowered the cups of her bra so that her breasts overlapped them, revealing her nipples so that he could suck on one while softly tickling the other. Bernice was near the point of climax off this alone, but she wanted, no, she needed to feel him inside her.

She was finally in the moment she'd been longing for. For months she'd been trying to get a piece of Derrick Goodwin, and now she had this man only instants always from swimming in her wetness. She closed her eyes and tilted her head back as Derrick's erection prepared to enter her- only it didn't.

Bernice opened her eyes, puzzled as to what had just happened to make Derrick stop. "Don't tell me you're having second thoughts again," she teased. "I promise it's worth your while."

But Derrick slowly started to back away. He placed his hardened penis back in his boxers and pulled up his pants. He grinned at Bernice and started to button back up his shirt. Bernice still didn't understand what had gone wrong so swiftly. After all, she'd gone through a hell of a lot to put this plan in motion so quickly. Her job was at risk if he decided to tell. Her pride was on the line if he decided to shame her. Her heart began to race.

She had come this far, she planned to follow through until the end, so she asked again, "Does dessert not appeal to you Derrick?"

"On the contrary," Derrick reassured, "the dessert is perfect." Bernice began to smile again, but Derrick continued, "Problem is, I like my dessert properly wrapped."

Bernice's eyes widened as she watched Derrick turn around, wink at her, and head back in the north wing break room. He gathered his lunch from the table and looked back at Bernice once more.

Shaking his head and mumbling under his breath, "Good God almighty..." he smiled again at Bernice and walked out.

Promises To Keep

Bernice stood up off the counter she was leaning on and rolled her eyes, pissed at herself for forgetting the one thing she needed to seal the deal.

How the fuck did you forget the condoms Bernie?!, she *silently yelled at herself.*

3
The Opposite Approach

"This is not a good look. I mean her claim is loaded. Did you see the report?"

"Yeah, I did. Isn't this his second lawsuit in three years?"

Two men walked up to the bathroom sink engaged in conversation. "Yup, two years ago it was the Simon case. We made that go away only for the fucker to get caught again. My God, what the hell is that stupid son of a bitch doing?"

"No doubt he's a dumbass, but he's a dumbass with a lot of power and a lot of money and this company isn't willing to risk either. I don't know why Jacob insists on fucking these teenagers for crying out loud. Women today are nothing like the women who worked for us when we were coming up through the ranks. Now, those were girls with common sense. They took these kinds of things as an opportunity to get ahead and get paid. And they shut up about it. Today's women just want to sue you. Pretty sad. This girl's case looks strong too."

"Oh yeah," the second guy agreed while brushing his hair in the mirror. "Jacob definitely has a fight with this one. He may not be able to buy his way out - assuming the right attorney is in the lead chair."

"And I bet you want that to be you. Ha! Well who knows what that prick Rich will decide. Hand me a piece of paper towel, will ya?" the first gentleman asked drying his hands before heading for the door. "You hungry? Come on let's grab some lunch."

The two men exited the bathroom and Derrick unlocked the stall he was quietly sitting in the entire time.

He recognized the men's voices as Mark Donaldson and Winston Cass, two older attorneys who had a knack for running their mouths and kissing Rich's ass to his face, while secretly dogging him to shit behind his back. He couldn't believe they didn't check to see if the bathroom was empty before breaking cardinal rule number one-discussing a case in public. Derrick overheard everything.

From the information Mark was spilling, Jacob West was being sued. West was owner and CEO of Jacob West & Co., the biggest accounting firm in New England and the biggest financial client of MEA. West represented

Broadway and Hollywood stars, sports figures, and radio personalities. Word on the street was that West was on the mob's payroll, but that had never been proven. According to Mark and Winston, it sounded like he was being sued for sexual harassment and this was huge news for Derrick.

Winning this case could be major to his future, that is, if he was given the case to begin with. It would finally show Rich who the real master attorney was in the firm, and he'd have no choice but to make him partner. The money and notoriety that would come along with being partner at MEA was all Derrick would need to finally start his own firm comfortably.

Derrick pulled out his cell phone to call Monica. For a split second, he had forgotten that Monica wasn't speaking to him right now. He was so excited to tell her the tea, but was quickly reminded of their status when she didn't answer.

Fuck, he screamed to himself. No matter how mad she'd gotten at him over the years, she didn't usually go this long without speaking. It had been two days. Derrick had to find a way to repair his friendship with her. But first, he needed to seek advice about how to get on this West case.

Walking down the hall past his office, he caught a glimpse at Bernice, who had already made her way back from the north wing. She was at the fax machine chatting with a couple other assistants. Derrick wasn't worried about her saying anything about their encounter. Number one, it was her idea and setup from the beginning. Number two, he had a feeling it wouldn't be their last. But he was glad Bernice didn't have any condoms. To him, women who carried condoms were women on the prowl for dick. He liked the chase. And yes Bernice was assertive in her approach, but he understood that it happened after all the other attempts had failed.

Derrick had a weakness for beautiful women and he wasn't oblivious to Bernice's previous advances. He knew all the times she invited him out were just her shooting her shot. And while he wasn't opposed to giving Bernice a taste at some point, he didn't think now was the best time, which is why he didn't inform her he had two condoms in his wallet. Derrick was always prepared for sex; he never left home without them.

He winked at Bernice subtly and she grinned without much attention from anyone else. Their gaze was quick and unnoticeable; Bernice never broke conversation with the assistants she was entertaining. Derrick continued down the hall to the elevator and headed up to the top floor. He needed to make his move on the West case and he knew he who he could turn to. He made his way up to the office of Joe Edwards.

Joe was a senior partner and had been at MEA since the doors opened many years ago. He and Rich Jr., the founder of the firm, were best friends at Boston College. As much as the company belonged to the McEnroe's, it belonged to Joe too. Joe wasn't as well off as Rich Jr. and didn't have the financial backings back then to invest in the firm. But now, at age 72, he was the oldest attorney in the company and he was loved and respected by everyone.

He was fair and honest, and he always had the firm's best interest at heart. He was well respected in courtrooms all over New England due to his track record as being open and ethical (which is something most people in the 80s didn't associate with being a defense lawyer), although he didn't litigate as often as he once did.

Joe was a short man in stature, about 5'7, sandy blond hair, what was left anyway, and his Boston accent was thick. Often times his voice reminded Derrick a lot of Joe Pesci's character in Goodfellas. Derrick was sold that there was some Italian roots somewhere in there, but nevertheless Derrick loved Joe, and Joe loved Derrick. He championed for him every time he could. He knew Derrick was capable of keeping the integrity of the firm that Rich Jr. envisioned intact, if given the chance. Despite his youthful mistake that almost got him disbarred, if no one else would ride for Derrick, Joe would.

Derrick saw Joe's door was open, so he knocked twice just to grab his attention. "You got some time for a brother?" he yelled inside the door.

Joe laughed. "Get in here you schmuck, of course I've got time." Joe stood up from behind his desk to walk over to greet Derrick. He shook his hand with his right hand and placed his left hand on Derrick's arm since he was too short to reach Derrick's neck. "Come, sit down," Joe instructed as they walked over to the couch near the window.

Joe's office still looked the way it probably did in 1978, just now it was more space to house more junk. He had his decanter of scotch in one corner, a record player in the other, a corduroy couch near the window, and a case filled with awards, medals, pictures, and degrees. His decor was old fashioned. He kept his cabinet dusted and a plastic cover over his couch. He even had a tie dye runner from his door to his desk where he insisted you walk. Joe could very well afford an upgrade, he just didn't want to. And at 72 years old, no one was going to make him either.

"What's on your mind kid?" Joe asked.

"Well," Derrick paused, "a birdie whispered in my ear about Jacob West and well… I want in."

"A birdie whispered?" Joe replied with a cutting side eye. "Ain't too many birds privy to that kind of intel."

Derrick knew Joe could see through the bullshit. He wasn't even sure why he tried to begin with, so he came clean. "Okay, I overheard it. But I wasn't eavesdropping. These two idiots were openly discussing it in the bathroom and not once did they check to see who was in there."

"Who?"

"Come on Joe, don't make me say names," Derrick pleaded. He knew he could get them in big shit if he said their names to Joe. Not that Joe would tell, but more so take matters into his own hands. Joe was a stickler for upholding the law and the rules, so hearing that two attorneys discussed a private case in a public bathroom grinded Joe's gears.

"If they were dumb enough to talk about a case in the shitter, then they deserve every bit of ass chewing they'll get from me. Now, who was it?" Joe asked again.

Derrick caved. "Mark and Winston."

"Ha!" Joe laughed. "Thing 1 and Thing 2? Bunch of bozos I tell you. They can't even chew gum and wipe their ass at the same time! Geez...I'll handle them later.

"But at any rate," Joe continued. "This case is going to be a whopper. This girl has some pretty hardcore evidence on Jacob and pretty soon if they don't come to a settlement, this will be public. So we've got to have our team in place before it does. Some of the partners will be heavily involved in his defense, but I agree that we need some young fresh litigants on this."

"Joe, you know I can do this. You saw what happened with the St. James case. All I need is the opportunity. I know Chris would approve, but Rich has been blocking me for months now. No way he's going to put me on this case."

"You goddamn right I'm not," said an unexpected voice from the door. Joe and Derrick turned to the door to find Rich standing in the threshold with his arms folded and his head tilted.

"This firm will not be turning over one of the biggest cases, and biggest threats to our company might I add, to you."

Derrick's blood pressure began to rise just at the sound of Rich's voice. The mere presence of Rich made his blood boil, but he was becoming more and more furious with every word that Rich spoke. Joe could see the fury flaming from Derrick and subtly motioned for him to relax.

"Now hold on there Rich, you just may want to take this into consideration," Joe reasoned. "As you yourself just said, this case is going to be one of the biggest this firm has ever seen and will be scrutinized under the microscope by every news media outlet in the nation. Derrick here has far more experience handling that kind of pressure given his work on the St. James case. It'd only make sense to add him as an assistant, if not lead counsel."

"Lead counsel?" Rich repeated before bursting out into laughter. "Are you drinking old man? There is no way in hell I'd make this boy lead counsel over anything."

"Boy?" Derrick echoed. He had tried to keep his composure with respect to Joe, but he'd had enough. He stood up, walked right up to Rich with his eyebrow raised, and he balled up his left fist at his side. There was no need to assume what Rich was alluding to with that use of that term and Derrick was 15 seconds away from dropping him where he stood.

"Who the hell are you calling 'boy'? I'm a grown ass man. A man who has made money for this firm time and time again. How many cases have I won? How many times have I proven myself to you and everyone else here? You know I deserve to be on this case. You know what I'm capable of."

"Besides fucking the D.A's witnesses, I'm not sure I do know what you're capable of Derrick," Rich countered, cutting Derrick off mid-sentence.

"ALRIGHT! Now that's enough!" Joe interrupted. He stared at Rich with deadly eyes as Rich wanted to continue speaking, but he knew Rich could tell playtime was over and he was done being the nice guy. "I said that's enough," Joe repeated.

Rich sat an envelope he was holding down on Joe's desk and preceded to leave, but before walking out the door, he made one last snarl at Derrick:

"Let's not forget I'm the reason you still can even practice law. You should be out on the street. So you don't get to come in here and tell me what cases you should or should not be working on. I don't care how much national attention you've gained or experience you have. Over my dead body will you be on this case representing McEnroe & Associates. And that's final. Good day, Joe," he said to the senior partner before departing the office.

Joe could feel the fumes radiating from Derrick; they shared the same sentiment. He disliked Rich just as much as Derrick and he hated the path Rich was leading the company down. Having been there from the beginning with Rich's father when the company was in its infancy stages, he desperately wanted someone else to take the reins who could bring the integrity and quality of service back to the firm. He knew Rich was not that guy, but what could he do. Chris wasn't strong enough to handle the day to day and he didn't expect Daddy McEnroe to leave the company to anyone else but his sons.

He glanced at Derrick, but he knew there was nothing he could say to subside the anger Derrick was feeling.

"I'm sorry kid. I know it sucks."

"Fuck him Joe. FUCK HIM AND FUCK MEA!" Derrick screamed before storming out of Joe's office. He was outraged at the level of disrespect he was just subjected to. He was done for the day. He needed to leave that building before he did or said something he would regret.

Promises To Keep

He stopped by his office to grab his briefcase and jacket and he didn't say a word to anyone, not even Bernice.

***

"I'll take a Crown Royal neat please."

"Coming right up," the bartender nodded.

Derrick walked over to the bar inside the Marriott across the street from the office to grab a drink and clear his head. He'd once again tried calling Monica and, like the last failed attempt, she didn't answer. It was driving him nuts that she wasn't responding. Monica was his confidant and best friend aside from being his lover. Between both Bernice and his boss trying to screw him, he needed her more than ever right now to help him sort things out. He could always count on Monica to calm him down when his temper was out of control. But since there was no Monica, he figured there was nothing a little Crown couldn't cure.

While waiting for his drink, he decided to shoot Monica a text; however, the moment he pulled out his phone it began to ring. Once he saw the name on the screen, he cringed. It was the last person he wanted to speak to at the moment, but he had to answer.

"Ugh, not now mom," he sighed before sliding the button green. "Good afternoon mom."

"Hey baby!" his mother responded gleefully. "How are you? I was afraid you weren't going to answer. You never have time for your momma lately."

"Sorry mom, just been busy with work."

"You're always busy with work- too busy. Can't you make time to stop by to see me? You know, I was thinking about making that beef stew you like."

"Mom… now isn't the best time," Derrick answered, "I'm really having a rough day and…"

"You know what, you're right," his mother said cutting him off in a disappointed tone. "It's okay. Now's not the best time. I'm sorry I bothered you. Just good to hear your voice."

Derrick sensed his mother was upset. He wasn't really trying to deal with his mother at the moment, but he also didn't want to upset her. So, he scaled back the attitude a bit, "Mom, listen. I'll come by one Saturday. We can have the beef stew then."

"Are you sure? I'd really like that. That would be perfect. You know I can't wait to see you sweetheart. Momma loves you."

Sighing under his breath, "I love you too mom. I'll talk to you later."

"Oh wait… before you hang up. Bring Monica. I haven't seen her in a while either and it would be great to see her pretty face. You know Derrick, she really is a nice girl. She would make a fine wife."

"Mom I don't want to get married. Come on, let's not do this."

"Let's not do what?" his mother asked switching her pitch from sweet to stern. Her Connecticut accent was strong and she was growing weary of waiting on Derrick to finally provide her a daughter-in-law or a grandchild. She always brought this conversation up when they spoke and she always mentioned Monica. Knowing her since she was a teenager, she'd always adored Monica and always felt Derrick was missing out on a good thing by not taking their relationship more serious.

"Monica is a good, smart girl," his mother continued, "and she's got a lot to offer a young man. Don't you let her get away from you being all stubborn."

"MOM!" Derrick screamed into the phone, "I am not going to marry Monica. See this... this is why I don't come around. I don't want to deal with this shit. Especially not right now."

Derrick's mom paused for a brief second. She was taken aback by his choice of language and aggressive tone. She felt her voice begin to shake when she tried to speak so she just decided not to say anything but goodbye.

"Well then. I guess it's time to cut this conversation short after all. I didn't raise you to talk to your mother that way. So I'll bid you a goodnight sir."

"Mo..." but it was too late. She'd hung up the phone and the damage had been done. He instantly regretted speaking to his mother that way. Talking to her just always made him irritable. She was so soft spoken and timid and for once in his life he wanted to see a fiery side of her. He didn't get his ability to stand up for himself from his mother that was for sure. He didn't see any characteristics of his mother in himself for that matter, and in many ways, he resented her for being that way. But today wasn't about his mom or her faint-hearted demeanor. He took out his anger at everything else on his mom just now and he recognized that was wrong. It would have been right to pick up the phone to call back and apologize. But he couldn't. And she was right about one thing: Monica would make a fine wife- just not his.

His thoughts drifted back to her and he finally shot her a text:

Mo, just got off the phone with mom. Of course she wants to see you. Beef Stew on Saturday?

He pressed send but instantly wished he hadn't. Monica had him tripping. If he didn't want to be with her, he needed to let it go, but that just wasn't Derrick. He got what he wanted and more when it came to women. Just the more he sat there, and the more shots he took, the more the realization of what was happening was setting in, I *may have really fucked up this time*, he thought to himself.

He downed another shot of Crown and drafted another message: Mo listen, I'm sorry. Please let's talk about this. I'm at the Marriott. Things at work are shitty and I really need you, Mo. I really need you. I miss you. Call me.

He was hoping to at least get a response if nothing else. He signaled for the bartender to pour him another drink and lazily lay his head on the bar. Derrick was just drained. It had been one of the craziest Monday's he could remember.

Suddenly, he heard the sound of someone sobbing. He lifted his head off the bar to notice a woman seated a few stools down to his left. Caught up in his own drama, he didn't even realize she was sitting there, but now that she had his attention, the sobs were becoming louder and louder. Maybe the drinks were starting to really take effect on him, because looking at her made his heart jump. He couldn't help but notice how strikingly beautiful she was.

She had shoulder length naturally curly brown hair and her legs were as smooth as the day was long. The black pencil skirt she was wearing was tightly hugging hips that barely fit on the barstool she was seated on. His eyes followed her legs down to the red bottom heels she was wearing. As she gazed straight through to the mirror that was behind the bar, Derrick looked at her face through the mirror's reflection. He could see her perfectly shaped brows, the voluptuousness of her lips that were covered in fire red lipstick, and the tears that fell from her hazel brown eyes.

When the bartender returned with Derrick's drink, Derrick motioned for him to give the lady to the left whatever she was drinking. When she received her drink, she looked down in Derrick's direction and raised her glass to signal thanks. Ordinarily, that would have been an opportunity to add a new beauty to his already very extensive roster of women, but today just wasn't the day.

He instead acknowledged her raised glass by raising his own and nodded to insinuate that the drink was on him. Derrick didn't want to come off as that guy whom a girl feels obligated to talk to once he buys her a drink, but he would have welcomed the conversation had she initiated it. Instead, the mystery woman continued to sit at the bar and sip her beverage, so Derrick continued to admire her from a far.

About fifteen minutes had passed and Derrick could see her periodically looking down to his end of the bar, yet Derrick remained steadfast in not being the first to make a move. He continued to sit there on his phone and look busy. He had already told the bartender when her Margarita was done to make sure she had another round, but it was time Derrick made his way home.

He stood up to grab his wallet and pulled out his card in an attempt to pay his tab, signaling for the bartender, who was entertaining the customers on the other end. The entire time he stood there, the woman at the bar stared at him with that elevator look- eyeing him up and down from the top of his head to the bottom of his feet. She watched him put on his jacket and right when he handed his card to the bartender, she stood from her stool with intentions to approach him.

Standing before him, even more beautiful up close than from a distance, she opened her mouth to speak. "Sorry to bother you, but it appears you're getting ready to leave, so I just wanted to say thank you for the drinks before you go."

He turned to face her, mesmerized by her beauty. "It was no problem at all, no thanks needed. I was just hoping to brighten someone else's day since mine has been super long and exhausting. So, just know that the pleasure was all mine."

She cracked a smile after just moments ago looking as if she hadn't smiled in ages. "I don't usually accept drinks from most men. They usually use it as a gateway to hit on me with the most tired lines I'd ever heard."

43

"Interesting. Does it usually work, cause I can order a few more," Derrick said jokingly.

After another margarita, another Crown neat, and quick chats about the weather, Derrick finally asked, "What's your name?"

"Destiny," she replied.

"Nice to meet you Destiny. I'm Derrick. Derrick Goodwin."

"Nice to meet you as well. I was really having a tough day- family problems. Just being able to take my mind off some things has really made me feel better, so thank you."

Derrick tried not to stare in her eyes, but he was captivated by everything about Destiny. Even her voice was calm and sexy, reminiscent of Gabrielle Union's in his opinion. He had an inner urge to take her right then and there on the bar, and he was becoming more and more turned on by just the look of her. He needed to get out of there before he was unable to control himself.

"Glad I was able to help. I had a rough day too, so this was good for me. Helped me clear my head," Derrick responded.

Destiny and Derrick stood up simultaneously. Their eyes were locked on each other. His hands were still on the bar. Her hands were still on her drink, closely grazing the side of his hand. For a second, it was like no one else was in the room for either of them. There was a connection in that moment that neither of them was able to understand how or why, but both of them felt it.

"Welp, I guess this is goodbye," Destiny said breaking the awkwardness of their gaze, "but again, it was nice to meet you and thanks."

"I guess it is," Derrick agreed giving Destiny a lecherous look, only to glance up and see the worse reflection he could have possibly seen in the bar's mirror glaring back at him.

He quickly broke the stare with Destiny and turned around to see Monica looking directly at him.

"Monica," Derrick began to explain, but she was not in the mood to hear it.

"No need to explain," Monica countered with a hurtful grin. "I knew you were full of shit. I fucking knew it."

"It's not what you think, really," Derrick pleaded. He had totally forgotten that he told Monica where he was and even still, she never responded that she was going to join him. He grabbed Monica's hand trying to find the right words to convince her not to leave. But internally, he also wanted to turn back to Destiny to tell her not to leave either. He could see her packing up her jacket and grabbing her bag. Derrick was torn, but not for long.

"Leave me alone Derrick… for good. I can't do this. I don't know how or when, but somewhere along the way I fell in love with you. And everyday I see signs that you'll never give me all of you and I just can't do this anymore," Monica stated before dropping Derrick's hand, backing away quickly and leaving him standing there.

"You may want to go after her," Destiny suggested after watching the spat from a distance.

"It's no use. I just keep screwing it up. See why I needed that drink?" Derrick replied.

Destiny placed her finger inside Derrick's hand, "One woman's trash is another woman's treasure. Never forget that."

Taking one more second to memorize her face, Derrick smiled and turned to walk away.

"Good day to you Ms. Destiny."

"And to you as well, Mr. Goodwin."

Meanwhile, Monica ran straight to the bathroom in the lobby, visibly upset about what she walked in on. She knew Derrick was being his same old 'always got to have a new piece of ass' self. She was tired of waiting for something she knew would never be. She saw all she needed to see with Derrick and said to herself this was definitely the final straw. She left the bathroom after wiping her nose, attempting to stop the tears before they began. She needed to get over being this sob ass softy of a person she'd become for Derrick and get back to being badass Mo. She exited the bathroom just in time to see Derrick heading to his car. He was alone surprisingly, but that didn't mean much. He could have easily gotten her number or business card or any other form of contact information. Monica wasn't fooled.

She continued out the bathroom, walking right past the front desk. She paused for a second. She had plans on gathering herself together and proceeding to her car, but not before she got a good glimpse at this woman who at least for the moment had Derrick's attention.

In the past, Derrick would always bring his girls around. Maybe he could sense that Monica was becoming less and less capable of standing the sight of them, but soon, it became more of a name and number association and less of name to face association. Monica was intrigued to know what it was he saw in this particular woman who had him stuck on stupid and eye ogling so hard that he didn't even notice her standing there staring at them both.

Destiny was standing at the front desk appearing to check in. Monica's eyes widened; she was certainly a familiar face.

I've seen her somewhere before, Monica murmured to herself, *but where?* Then a light switch clicked on in her head. She smirked at her thoughts. She remembered.

Promises To Keep

4
Office Visit

From his secretary secretly seducing him in an abandoned location, to him and his boss having a flat out verbal assault in a senior partner's office, right before meeting a mysterious woman at the bar, only to have Monica catch him, Derrick felt this day would go down in infamy as the worst day ever. He couldn't remember a day where he had such a rollercoaster of emotions. He didn't like the feeling of not being in control and it was apparent that he wasn't in control of any of the day's events.

Standing in front of the fridge, he moved all the fruits, veggies, and left over take out boxes out of the way so he could access the wine. He usually reserved the Chardonnay for when he was having female company, but it seemed appropriate to crack it open after the day's highs and lows.

Derrick took a stemless wine glass from the cabinet, poured his first glass, and guzzled it without taking a breath. He sighed deeply, as if the wine was slowly releasing the weight he carried. He poured another after another until eventually he grabbed the half drank bottle and headed into the living room.

It was unusually quiet in his apartment. The place was usually either filled with Will Downing records playing while Derrick studied a case, or the sound of someone's daughter moaning in the bedroom. But more often than not, you could usually hear Monica's laughter resonating through the apartment.

Every encounter wasn't a sexual one; they were friends before anything. They would watch Martin reruns together, sing along to cable karaoke, and assist in each other's cases - whether one asked for help or not. It was bugging Derrick more than he cared to let on that Monica wasn't around. While it had only been two days since he originally pissed her off, it felt like an eternity. He couldn't remember the last time he'd missed someone so genuinely. And with everything going on at work, not having Monica was like not having his confidant. He couldn't believe he was stupid enough to get caught up. But after he took a few more drinks, coupled with the slight buzz he had from the bar earlier, his mood began to change. Depression turned to indifference.

"She didn't even let me explain," he said aloud. "And if anyone should be mad it should be me. She's not my girl. And I wasn't even doing shit wrong. Shit, I was just talking to her. I should have kept on talking to her."

He continued to convince himself that he had done nothing to deserve the treatment he got from Monica with every sip of wine he took. And the less he thought about Monica, the more he began to fantasize about Destiny.

"Hell, she looked better than Monica anyway. That's probably why she was mad," he said laughing and intoxicated. "Fuck her. Shit, she knew what this was."

Derrick finished the entire bottle of chardonnay and was looking for more. When he realized it was his only bottle, he decided a beverage change was in order. He headed straight for the liquor cabinet.

Monica had mentioned to Derrick several months back that inebriation had become the way he handled problems as of late. Of course, Derrick denied that he ate when he was stressed and he drank when he was unable to confront his feelings. He'd often joke with her that he was going to need AA before he was 30. However, at times, it didn't seem like a joke to Monica.

Derrick would never admit he was developing a habit of drinking to feel better. But in this moment, he realized he had nothing and no one else to turn to. He wasn't a man with many male friends and the one homeboy he linked up with often, Dray, was out of town. He found solace in the purple bag that was sitting full in his cabinet.

Cracking open the Crown Royal, he poured up a rocks glass and sipped the night away until he passed out right on the couch.

***

"I'll tell you, I've been looking over this file for days now and I still can't understand how the circuit court came up with this ruling. I'll give it a couple more glances but… hold on a sec. Yes Christy?"

"Sorry to bother you Mr. Goodwin, but you have someone here to see you regarding a consultation."

"A consultation?" Derrick said with confusion. He placed his call on hold with clear frustration on his face. This had to be Rich up to his tricks again.

"Christy, there must be some mistake. Give me one second."

Christy was a temp filling in for Bernice while she was taking a vacation. She wouldn't have any idea that the paralegals and first year associates on the third floor handled all the consultations. Whoever it was had to be sent by Rich as another way to throw his weight around. Derrick was sick of it.

He advised her to send the potential client downstairs. "Christy, please send the client down to the third floor and apologize for the mix up. All consultations will be taken care of by the associates there. I don't have time right now. I'm actually on the line with a very important client, and would prefer to not be disturbed."

"But Mr. Goodwin, she asked specifically for you."

"She," Derrick mumbled to himself.

Bernice set up his schedule before she left a little over a week ago, after their rendezvous in the break room. He didn't recall setting up any appointments, certainly not any consultations. His first thought was maybe it was Monica trying to surprise him since he hadn't spoken to her since last Monday. But Monica was well known around the office, and she wouldn't have to sneak in on him. In fact, she wouldn't have even stopped by the secretary's desk; she would have just walked her ass on in.

Derrick was now intrigued with who this mysterious woman was and why she specifically, with no appointment, wanted to consult with him.

"Alright," he replied to Christy, "send her in."

Using his earpiece to continue his previous conversation, Derrick stood at the window looking out over the Hartford skyline. He heard the door open and the clicking of heels behind him. So he turned around to see who the mysterious consultation was and almost shit a brick when looked upon her face in his office.

"Hey… let me give you a follow up call once I know more…. Okay. Thanks again… Goodbye." Derrick ended that call faster than a fat kid chasing an ice cream truck.

"Destiny?"

"I see your memory serves you well," she responded.

"How could I forget? Although I must admit I definitely didn't expect to see you walking through my office door. Matter of fact, how did you even know I worked here?"

Destiny giggled. "I mean come on, you're Derrick Goodwin. Name a person in this city who doesn't know you or where you work."

Derrick chuckled. "Oh am I that popular now?" he asked as he walked closer towards her. "You didn't seem to notice my popularity the day we met."

"I don't always play my hand at once. But I knew who you were."

"That's interesting. So what other cards are you holding from me?" Derrick replied flirtatiously. He sat at the edge of his desk directly in front of her. She looked even more stunning today than she did when they met at the bar. He was happy to see her – almost too happy.

Gawking, his eyes began to wander from her face to her breasts and back to her face. He watched her lips move as she spoke. Her curly hair was pinned to the right side of her head, which gave Derrick a better image of her left side profile and neckline. Her white blouse and black waist pants hugged her in all the right places. She was once again wearing that hypnotizing red lipstick and it was difficult for Derrick to pay attention to anything other than how extremely breathtaking she was.

"My God you are beautiful," Derrick accidentally said aloud. He immediately regretted it after looking upon the discomfort in Destiny's face.

"While I appreciate the compliment, I want to keep this visit strictly professional and I don't want to be misleading on why I'm here. The other day at the bar, I believed you to be professional and a gentleman, not like everyone else. Was I wrong?" She dropped her head to look at floor.

Embarrassed, Derrick quickly offered an apology for his outburst. "I honestly didn't mean to offend you Destiny, and for that I truly apologize. I would be a liar to say that I don't find you very attractive, but you are correct. It was very unprofessional of me to let my thoughts get in the way like that and I hope you'd allow me a chance to offer you the help you came here for. "

Destiny softened her expression, raising her face to meet his, "Apology accepted."

She stood up and began to pace the office, prefacing the reason for her visit. "It's been hard these least few weeks to decipher whom I can and can't trust. But something about you Derrick says I can totally trust you. Can I trust you?"

"Well, I'm a lawyer Destiny... I think that's your answer," Derrick replied chuckling, but this annoyed her further. She wasn't really in the playing mood and was starting to feel like she wasn't being taken seriously.

"You know what, this was a bad idea. It's okay. I'll seek advice from someone else. Thanks for your time."

"Whoa! Hold on now," Derrick said caringly as he rushed over to stop her from walking out of his office. He softly grabbed her arm and closed the door she was attempting to open. He turned her around to face him, before once again offering an apology for his insensitive behavior.

"Please," Derrick said. "Don't leave."

Promises To Keep

Destiny walked to the chair she was just sitting in and placed her bag down. Without warning, she turned back to Derrick, wrapping her arms around his neck and began kissing him assertively. Derrick was caught off guard by her untimely gesture, but soon met her passion, pulling her in closer to him and locking his lips with hers.

Seconds into their moment of lust, Destiny began ripping off Derrick's blazer. She unbuttoned his shirt, exposing his chest and began to place soft sensual kisses sporadically on his body. She pushed him back on his desk while unbuckling her pants and kicking off her shoes.

Tossing the items to the floor, Derrick lay across his desk on his back allowing Destiny to straddle him. She had removed her pants already, revealing to Derrick that she wasn't wearing any underwear. Her womanhood was smooth and bare, just the way Derrick liked it.

Her kitty was purring for his attention and he was ready to give it to her. Once Destiny climbed on top of him, he motioned for her to slide her body up higher, placing her folds directly above Derrick's lips. Answering her kitty's call, Derrick slowly used his tongue to gently outline the outer rim of her lower lips before inserting his tongue into her sweet spot.

Destiny moaned with delight. With every touch of Derrick's tongue, her body shook until she reached her breaking point. Her attempts to be quiet failed, and the closer she came to her climax, the louder her screams became. Derrick could feel her body pulsating. He closed his eyes and sped up his tongue strokes to match her movements. Destiny could no longer contain herself. She yelled his name in accession, "Derrick… Derrick… DERRICK!"

Derrick opened his eyes hoping to see Destiny well pleased after his oral treatment. But instead, he found Destiny seated across from his desk waiting on him to provide an answer to a question she had apparently just asked.

"Derrick?" he heard her say again. "Do you understand?"

"Uh yeah," Derrick answered, "I got you." *What the fuck?* he thought to himself. *What the hell just happened?*

"Good," Destiny affirmed. "You know, for a moment there I felt like you were daydreaming or something."

"I'm fine," Derrick replied. "So, how about you tell me why you're here."

Destiny took a deep breath and lowered her head for a split second. She looked to be a bit embarrassed by what she was about to say and Derrick could sense she was uncomfortable.

"Listen, you can tell me. Judgment free zone here. What's wrong?"

"I need a lawyer because I want to sue my employer."

"My assistant said you needed a consultation. Seems like you already have in your mind that you want to sue, so before I can agree to take your case, I just need to know more. Why are you looking to sue?"

Destiny inhaled deeply before opening up to Derrick about her situation: "Okay. My boss has been making me feel uncomfortable for months. I have emails from him asking me out and telling me how much he loves to see my legs when I wear skirts to work. He's promised to give me things in exchange for sex, which I decline every time. And I've even been threatened to be publicly shamed if I ever said anything. He's not touched me in anyway, but he's the older type. The kind that makes you feel like you asked for it by how you dress or how you speak."

Derrick's face turned as red as Destiny's lipstick that he loved so much. He had no explanation as to why, but to hear that someone was trying to take advantage of Destiny instantly upset him. "I'm sorry to hear this is happening. Have you tried to report his behavior to human resources?"

Destiny sarcastically laughed, "Ha! You try reporting sexual harassment on the owner of the company and see how far you get. Besides, the other accountants who've filed a report eventually ended up fired. I don't need that to happen to me. I need my job. This is why I'm in a bind. Before I continue to pursue this, I need other opinions on if I have a strong case. Will I win?"

"Whoa. Hold up. You're an accountant?" Derrick repeated.

"Yes. Why? What's the problem?"

"Destiny, who exactly do you work for?"

Destiny looked directly into Derrick's eyes and said the exact two words he was praying she would not say, "Jacob West."

Derrick was fucked. He knew it. He knew she was going to say the one guy he couldn't technically sue. He was pissed, but he had to break the news.

"Destiny, I don't know how to say this, but Jacob West is one of this firm's biggest clients. We're already representing him on this case."

"Really?" Destiny replied in disbelief.

"This sucks. And I wish this wasn't the way it works, but unfortunately for me that means representing you would be a conflict of interest and highly unethical. I'm really sorry, but I can't take your case."

Destiny tilted her head and squinted her eyes at Derrick. Her face carried a look of disappointment and Derrick could feel her cutting through him with her gaze.

"You know, if you didn't want to be my lawyer, all you had to do was say so and not make up shit," Destiny finally spoke.

"Excuse me?"

"How can you already be handling Jacob's case against me when I haven't filed anything yet. I don't have a case. I just told you I want to know if I'll win first before going through with anything."

"Wait…" Derrick stuttered. "You don't already have an established case that you've prepared regarding West's behavior? You said 'other opinions' as if you've disclosed this info to someone else."

"No!" Destiny repeated as she grabbed her bag. "How can I have a case against him when I can't event report this shit to HR. I came here hoping to secure a lawyer to begin working on a case and steer me in the right direction. I came here to secure you because I heard you were the best at this."

"Destiny, I am very good at what I do, but this is a clear conflict of interest. I want to help, I really do, but I can't help in this way."

Destiny's eyes began to water. She was visibly upset and disheartened. "Well, thank you for your time Mr. Goodwin. I guess with him being 'your client' you're right. You can't help me. Shame. I thought you were one of the good guys. But I guess you're like every other white-collar man who would rather save his own, even if it were a disgusting pig, than do some good. Sorry I wasted your time." Destiny stood up and headed for the door.

"Destiny. Don't walk away feeling like that. It's not the case. I promise you, it's not like that. "

"Okay…"

"I'm really sorry."

Destiny turned to Derrick with tears in her eyes and firmness in her voice, "Don't be."

She walked out the door, slamming it behind her.

5
Inside Scoop

Derrick badly wanted to run after Destiny. Seeing her tear up did something to him emotionally. Knowing that a slime ball like West was harassing her and there was nothing within his power he could do about it also got under his skin. He couldn't explain why Destiny made him feel this way, but there was a connection with her that he hadn't felt with any other woman. It was different than the connection he had with Monica. He had been thinking about her for over a week and she finally showed up in his office asking for help that he couldn't provide. No. There had to be a way. He was determined to find out how he could be there for Destiny without breaking legal ethics. He would move heaven and earth to make her feel better and to not ever see her cry again.

He sat down behind his desk trying to process the information Destiny had just given him. Derrick was sure he could think of a suitable solution, so he took out his legal pad and began to jot down a few notes:

- Has emails saved of gifts for sexual favors
- Job security threatened
- Going on for months
- Fear led to silence
- ? vs. Jacob West. WHO?

Suddenly, it hit Derrick how he could help Destiny, but his idea would only work if he knew who the plaintiff was in the current case against West. He knew that it wasn't public record as of yet because the case had not been officially filed; hence why Winston and Mark were complete idiots for discussing such a private case so publicly. But, Derrick wasn't going to just be able to walk into Rich's office and find out the details. Aside from the fact that Rich hated Derrick's guts, he made it very clear that Derrick was not going to be sitting on the case and in these types of cases, only sitting attorney's would be able to view the case files until the case was officially filed for public record.

Derrick sat at his desk for a moment pondering what kind of plan he could devise to get the name he needed.

Then it came to him. He knew exactly who could get that information for him, but it would come at a cost. For Destiny, it was a price he was willing to pay.

"Christy," he called to his temporary assistant.

"Yes Mr. Goodwin?" she responded via telecom.

"Hold my calls for today. Cancel my meetings. I've gotta cut out early."

"Surely sir."

Derrick grabbed his suit jacket, his phone, and his tie, and headed for the door. As he made his way to the elevator, he unlocked his phone and opened his contacts. He scrolled and scrolled until he got to the number he wanted, and sent a text: I need to see you; it's an emergency. Can you make time?

Before hitting send, Derrick paused. He stared at his phone, pacing the elevator that he occupied alone, second-guessing on whether or not he really wanted to send this message. He then remembered Destiny's mascara filled tears leaving his office, and his decision was made.

"Fuck it," Derrick said aloud.

Message sent.

***

Derrick pulled up in front of a two story multifamily home on the south end of Hartford. He could smell the cultural mix of Adobo and Sazón seasoning in the air and could hear the salsa music that was blasting from a few houses down. Hartford was known for its diversity and the south end was where most Puerto Ricans and Dominicans dwelled. The area wasn't the roughest in town, but it was no suburb either. Nevertheless, he had a goal to get the name of the plaintiff in the West case and he knew being there would achieve that. He sent a text announcing his arrival.

He saw the door open seconds after the text was sent. He took a deep breath and exited the car. He was nervous. Not at what he was about to do, but at why he was about to do it.

As he walked up the steps, his nose began to smell an aroma of familiarity: a tropical blend of coconut oil and a delicious dark skinned black woman. He knew he was at the right place. And as he approached the door, his eyes confirmed what his nose had already concluded.

"I see you're enjoying your paid vacation," Derrick said flirtatiously while closing the front door behind him.

"It's been okay, but I have a feeling it's about to get a whole lot better."

It was Bernice. Derrick walked in to see her sitting on her couch in a thin red and gold kimono type housecoat, sipping on a glass of white zinfandel. He found it hard to believe that she would just randomly be half naked sipping wine at 2:00 in the afternoon; however, if her goal was to get Derrick's full attention, she succeeded.

"I was quite shocked to get your text asking to stop by," Bernice began, "you've never seemed interesting in stopping by before. To what do I owe the pleasure Mr. Goodwin?"

"Mr. Goodwin? I think we're past the formalities at this point and considering this isn't the office, Derrick will do just fine."

"Whatever you prefer, Derrick," giggled Bernice. "Still haven't answered my question, yet. What's the emergency that couldn't wait until my vacation was over?"

Derrick, being the gentleman he was, was still standing at the door since he had not yet been offered a seat. Gesturing towards the couch, "May I?" he asked.

"By all means," Bernice answered, crossing her legs sensually, allowing room for Derrick to be seated.

Derrick was there for a purpose, but Bernice was stunning in her comfort. Her skin glowed, as if she had sunrays following in her shadow. Her slim legs were oiled perfectly and glistened by the light shining in from the window. Her housecoat was tied very loosely at the waist, exposing her white bra and suspenders from her garter belt, though she wasn't wearing any stockings or thigh highs to attach them.

As he sat beside Bernice, he could feel his body temperature rising. He hadn't even mentioned why he was there yet, but he was already unloosening his tie. Bernice silently laughed. She could see temptation was getting the best of him. It was written all over his face. And while she missed one opportunity to bed Derrick, she would not allow another one to pass her by. She knew what she doing. And quite frankly, she didn't care why he was there.

Bernice had one goal and one goal only: to fuck Derrick Goodwin. And now he was sitting in her house, on her couch, needing her for a favor. She'd do whatever he asked of her anyway because he was her boss and a damn good one. But she'd do it expeditiously if the dick was bomb. And she was tired of waiting, so she uncrossed her legs and shifted her body to face Derrick. As she turned, her housecoat opened even further, permitting Derrick to get a full glance of what she had to offer.

"Can I get you some water?" Bernice offered. "You seem a little warm."

"It's definitely hot in here," Derrick replied, "but I don't think water is what I'm thirsting for."

Scooting herself closer to Derrick, Bernice untied her housecoat, and dropped it slowly to her shoulders, exposing her body completely.

Shit, Derrick thought to himself, as he uncontrollably leaned in heatedly to kiss Bernice. Wrapping her arms around Derrick, matching his fire, Bernice leaned backwards on the couch, turning her face away and allowing Derrick to begin to set a trail of kisses from her cheek, down to her neckline and onto her breasts. He took them both into his hands, massaging them in a circular motion, using his thumbs to slightly tickle her nipples. Bernice sighed with pleasure while unstrapping her bra to get the full sensation of Derrick's touches.

With full access to her C-cup mounds, Derrick assertively sucked each one, heightening Bernice's craving to feel him inside her. She was becoming increasingly moist with each touch and Derrick's pants could no longer sustain the arousal building up between his legs. He unbuckled his pants while Bernice slipped off her panties. Grabbing her garter belt to remove it, Derrick seized her arm and stopped her.

"Oh no baby… Leave it," he said erotically. Bernice obliged.

Derrick flipped Bernice over on her stomach, preparing her for doggy style, which was his favorite position. Her ass was rounded to perfection and as Derrick slid on the condom that he'd gotten from his pants pocket, he raised her bottom to meet his erection and gradually entered into her pool of wetness.

Slowly, with his hands on her waist, he guided her body back and forth over his shaft. He wasn't expecting her to be this wet or to feel this good, but Bernice's sweetness was like a faucet with a leak that never stopped dripping. The better it began to feel, the faster Derrick sped up his movements, until finally he found a rhythm that soothed the itching Bernice had to feed him. Her head was tilted all the way back, biting her lips as she moaned in delight. She begged Derrick not to stop.

"Oh yes… God, don't stop. Don't stop. Ah…"

Derrick's ego grew with every word she spoke, encouraging him to go harder and speak louder. "This dick feels good to you, huh baby?"

"Yes… yes," Bernice uttered with each stroke.

Derrick thought he had her right where he wanted her. His plan was to pipe her good enough to do anything he asked, including getting the name of the plaintiff from the files at work that he couldn't access because he wasn't assigned to the case.

Bernice was at the point of no return. "I'm gonna cum! I'm gonna cum!"

When Derrick heard that, he took extra steps to ensure this climax reached its full potential. He licked his fingers and began to rapidly rub her clit, elevating her climax to new heights, while he continued to pound her from behind. Bernice enjoyed the roughness of it all and could no longer hold on. It was only a matter of seconds until Derrick could see her juices all over him and the condom. When he felt her body weaken, he decided it was his turn to release. He was the type who always wanted to make sure his partner came first. He grabbed a hold of the back of the couch and exploded inside of her.

"Ah... Shit," Derrick called out as he bust. He fell back onto the couch where they both lay, semi-exhausted, yet satisfied from the performance of the other.

"My God, Derrick Goodwin," Bernice finally spoke breathing heavily, "you are one helluva lover. Guess the rumors are true."

"They usually are," Derrick smirked. He was well aware of what women said about him. He wasn't pressed over gossips. But he knew fucking him was something Bernice had been waiting to do since their last encounter in the north wing of the office, and as good as the pussy was, he couldn't lose sight of what he was there for. Now was the time to make his request.

"Seems your circle talks a lot at the office. Have they by chance been talking about the Jacob West case?"

"Ohhhh, so that's it!" Bernice gathered.

"What?"

"You came to see me about the Jacob West case."

"Well, not exactly. Indirectly. Well, what I'm saying is you're well connected with the other assistants, right?"

"Something like that."

"Well, I believe your connection with Rich's assistant, Connie, could get me much needed information on the case. I think I have a really good lead, but I need to know who the plaintiff is."

"But why do you need me for that? It's public record," Bernice countered.

"Not exactly. The case hasn't been entered into public record yet, so right now, the only people with access to the files are the attorneys on the case and their assistants. Since no attorney has officially been assigned, that means Rich is the only one with real access. Him and whomever he tells, which is not and will not be me."

"I see. And curiously, what do I get in return for my services?"

Derrick smiled, "You know that little thing that we just did?"

"Uh huh," Bernice responded.

"It gets better."

Bernice's eyes lit up. She wasn't even expecting to get more of Derrick, but she wasn't going to turn him down either. "Consider it done."

Boom, Derrick thought, *mission accomplished.*

Upon getting dressed and leaving, he kissed Bernice goodbye on the cheek. He was ecstatic about the progress he'd made in putting his plan into action, but then reality set in.

Once in the car, Derrick looked at himself in the overhead mirror, wondering what the hell he had just done. He enjoyed every bit of fucking Bernice, but damn, since when did he start sleeping with women to get information? And more importantly, when he did start going to great lengths for women he barely even knew? He felt out of character and yet, at the same time, he felt he owed it to Destiny to go above and beyond to help her. He could still see the disappointment in her face when she left his office earlier that day and now that he had an idea to help her, he needed to find her to tell her.

6
Charades

Destiny sat at the first booth near the window inside Black Eyed Sally's in Downtown Hartford. As she sipped her Blue Hurricane cocktail, she stared out the window onto the streets of Hartford, listening to the live blues band playing in the background and thinking about the many times she'd walked by this very restaurant wishing she could enjoy what it had to offer. She loved the New Orleans inspired décor of the restaurant. It had always been a dream of hers to travel to the Big Easy, and somehow sitting at that booth allowed her to think about what she would do if she could ever walk Bourbon Street or tour the French Quarters.

Promises To Keep

Destiny was born and raised in Hartford and had never been outside the state of Connecticut other than to visit some family in upstate New York. She worked harder than her older brother and her younger sister, yet as the middle child, she often felt the most alone, the most unaccomplished, the most burdened, and the most disappointing.

She often wondered how different her life would have been had she been blessed with a more stable childhood. Her mother did the best she could by her three children, but it wasn't nearly enough. They often went to bed hungry, and that's if they went to bed at all. Too often they sometimes missed the cutoff for a space in the Center, a women and children's shelter, and had to spend the night wherever her mother deemed the safest. For Destiny, closing your eyes in an unknown place three to four times a week could be challenging and soon, sleeping became more a luxury than a necessity.

Destiny's mother was an alcoholic. She drank from sun up to sun down, to the point where it had become the norm for Destiny and her older brother Devon to come in from school and find her mother on the kitchen floor unconscious and her baby sister Dera in her high chair screaming to the top of her lungs. Destiny was six years old when her family was evicted for lack of rental payment after her mother was fired for repeatedly showing up to work inebriated. She could never forget the embarrassment of seeing boards on her doors, her clothes and shoes on the front yard, her toys in a box, and her mom's furniture on the curb. They hadn't just been evicted, they were literally put out.

Oddly enough, in a moment that would have driven most alcoholics to go off the deep end, it was in that moment that her mother came to the realization that her problem compromised the life of her children.

Now on the streets with a two-year-old toddler, a six-year-old daughter, and an eight-year-old son, Destiny's mom quit drinking cold turkey. They stashed their belongings and furniture in an abandoned garage not too far from their old house, which was essentially where they laid their heads for a while. But after a couple months, as the Hartford nights turned colder and colder, it became an insufficient place to live with a baby. They had to find shelter. Destiny had two uncles in Syracuse, New York that welcomed them with open arms, but the financial cost was too steep, and the emotional cost was steeper.

Destiny's uncles were loving - too loving. And Destiny's mother wanted to make sure that the love between her daughters and their uncles had boundaries, unlike the lack thereof in her own childhood. She didn't want her daughters to face the same humiliation and shame that came along with being molested by your family, nor did she want her son to be under that kind of influence; therefore, the first time she saw her brother wink his eye at Destiny, she gathered their things and left. She would rather face the struggle of the Hartford streets than to subject her children to the kind of pain she endured growing up.

Promises To Keep

That kind of upbringing can drive a girl to do the unimaginable and as Destiny sat in that window staring out onto the downtown scene, she thought about the fair share of battles she fought to survive. If she had to steal, no sweat, she'd steal. If she had to lie, she'd do it in a heartbeat. And if she had to sleep with someone (male or female) to eat or pay the bills, then point her in the direction of the quietest room so she could handle her business and get her coins. She was a hustler in every sense of the word, but she also grew very tired of that life.

After finishing high school at High School Inc., an alternative school in Hartford, she knew college was her way out. She was much smarter than her grades suggested, but homework wasn't always at the forefront of your mind when you've spent the night before with your ass in the air to make a couple dollars for your graduation dress. Destiny decided community college would be a good, affordable start. She enrolled in Capital Community College to earn an associates degree in accounting. She figured if she knew how to handle money, she'd be able to make a lot more of it.

For two years, almost daily, she took that #64 bus that stopped right in front of Black Eyed Sally's. Every day that she waited at that bus stop, she'd daydream about when she'd be able to dine there. She was envious of the customers she'd seen enter more than once.

Must be nice to be regulars at such a place, she'd thought. But, it motivated her. She promised herself she'd get to become a Black Eyed Sally's regular too. And she did.

Now every time she came, she'd sit in the same window booth so that she could maybe provide some hope to someone else waiting for the bus, and for their breakthrough.

However, this visit was for a different purpose. This visit to her favorite restaurant was more business than pleasure. She was waiting for someone to arrive, but who she did not know.

A couple weeks prior, Destiny was approached by a man with a package. The package contained a letter - more like a script actually - and $5,000 cash. Her instructions were simple and the reward for her follow through was a hard bargain to turn down. After she had completed her mission, she was to shoot a text to the number at the bottom of the letter and wait for someone at her favorite restaurant. Destiny had never disclosed what her favorite restaurant was and yet not 10 minutes after being there did she see her business date arrive, or so she assumed.

Destiny slightly lifted her hand to get the attention of the person standing at the hostess stand who was wearing dark shades and a black cap. She couldn't tell if it was a man or woman from the distance, but she deduced from the height and the way the person sort of sashayed towards the table that it was a female. Approaching Destiny's table, the person looked around seemingly to see if anyone was watching them.

"Did you have to choose the booth directly in front of the window? This isn't the most discrete you know and discretion is the key to all of this."

"First off, you asked to meet me at my favorite place. I don't eat here if I can't sit in my favorite spot, which is this one, so deal with it," Destiny snapped back. "Secondly, I don't know you and not sure that I care to, but I do want to know what the hell is going on, how did you know I'd even be here, and are you the person who sent me that envelope, or you just some other pawn in this game I'm apparently playing?"

"Did you get the money?"

"Yes," Destiny answered.

"Then don't worry about who I am. Who I am matters not to you. The only thing that matters is that you follow instructions as given, which you obviously did or I wouldn't be here either."

Destiny realized this was definitely a woman. The attitude exuding from her pores was certified bitch, and that kind of bitch was one only a female could convey. But Destiny wasn't afraid to hold her own with this anonymous person who clearly had not done enough of a background check if she thought she was going to speak to Destiny that way.

"Why doesn't it? If you're involved in some illegal shit then I think I have the right to know!" Destiny exclaimed.

"Destiny, look. Let's not do this. You agreed to follow through with this plan the moment you took the money out that envelope. And I will follow through with my side of the deal. But you better lower your fucking voice in here."

Destiny hated to admit it, but she had a point. While she hadn't spent the money yet, she had plans for it, and those plans didn't involve returning the funds. So Destiny piped down. But only enough to get some clarity on what exactly she was getting herself into.

"Fine." Destiny conceded, "but seriously, who are you? And why me? Why I am the person to do this?"

"Uh," the woman sighed. "You just don't stop do you? Okay, fine. Let's just say I'm the bringer of justice and the teacher of lessons. And right now, it's time to teach Derrick Goodwin a lesson."

"And exactly what gives you the authority to teach anyone a lesson? Oh let me guess, he fucked your brains out and left you stranded on the side of the road like a mangy dog and now you're mad?"

"Oh, you're little tough girl act is cute," the woman replied unbothered by Destiny's insults. "But I don't think Derrick knows me. In fact, I know he doesn't know me at all," the woman said firmly with her head facing towards the window. You could tell she was gazing even though catching a glimpse of her eyes were impossible through her dark shades. But she swiftly snapped out her trance and turned her attention back to Destiny and the matter at hand.

"So, did he take the bait or not? What was his reaction?"

Rolling her eyes and showing reluctance to answer, Destiny finally decided to cooperate. "His reaction was exactly as the letter said it would be. He told me he couldn't help me because of some ethical conflict of interest or whatever. I rubbed it in, made him feel like shit for not agreeing to help me, and walked out. And yes, he hit on me as the letter implied he would. So I guess it's fair to say things went according to plan."

Destiny witnessed a devious smirk come across the woman's face as she sat back in the booth and folded her arms. It made Destiny feel even more uncomfortable and nervous than she already felt. Destiny was no stranger to schemes, but she usually knew the schematics of the plan and the purpose for the setup. In this case, she knew nothing. She was blind. Coerced into a plan she didn't understand and that made her very uneasy.

"Okay, so what's the next move?" Destiny asked.

"Call him, leave him a voicemail. Tell him you were too harsh, you understand his position, and that you want to meet up to apologize. "

"No, not with Derrick," Destiny interjected, "with Devon."

"Seriously?"

"Yes, seriously. I did what you asked and now your part of the plan is in motion. I want to know how you're planning on delivering on what you promised me in the letter," Destiny said firmly.

"You need to get one thing straight: I don't work for you, you're working for me. I'm the Boss."

Standing up to slide out of the booth the woman continued, more snarky with each word she spoke: "You don't get to ask me questions. You think I haven't done my homework on you, Ms. Destiny? Think I don't know where you come from and all your dirty little secrets? I know all about you. How do you think I knew this was your favorite place? Do you really want to try me? You really want to find out what I'm capable of? I don't think you do. So it would behoove you, if you want my assistance and the rest of the money promised to you, to just do what the fuck I tell you. You do that, you don't have to worry about me working on my part of the deal. You just better rethink your responses and your tone and do as you're told. Are we clear?"

Destiny dreadfully nodded in agreement. She was downright scared at this point and was fighting the tears forming in the corner of her eyes. This woman meant business and could sense Destiny's fear.

"Relax. Everything is fine. You just do your part and let me handle the rest. Now, as I was saying, you need to reach out to Derrick. If you stormed out his office the way you claim you did, then he's killing himself trying to come up with a way to help you. It's in his nature. Besides, he can't help himself with beautiful women. And beautiful women can't help themselves around him. So this should be a piece of cake."

"And where exactly should I tell him I want to meet?"

"You're a smart girl, Destiny… just make it happen."

The chick pulled out a couple hundred-dollar bills from her pocket and left it on the table. The two looked at each other briefly, Destiny still unable to see past her glasses or make out her face. She wore no earrings, had no identifiable shape, and wore a durag to mask her hair underneath her ball cap. She didn't have a young voice, nor one of an elder. Destiny had no clue who this woman was and couldn't alert anyone if she wanted to. Who would she describe? The woman in black or the woman who wanted her to screw over Derrick for reasons unknown? Destiny stared back at this mystery woman fearfully, knowing she didn't have a clue how much this woman knew about her or her family. She was obligated to follow through and she knew this woman knew that as well.

The Boss grinned devilishly while slowly backing away, eventually turning around and walking out of the restaurant. Once she could no longer see her, Destiny let out the air she didn't realize she was holding in during her death stare down with the mystery woman. She finished the last of her drink, collected her composure, and grabbed her bag off the seat. She opened her phone as she walked out of the restaurant, looking around to see if maybe she could see the unknown person she just met get into a car or something. But there was no one there in either direction. Destiny got to her car in the parking lot across from the restaurant and searched her contacts for Derrick's office number.

She was hesitant.

She liked Derrick. From the moment she met him in the bar, she felt he was different. She could tell he had his way with the ladies, but he was so easy to talk to, and he certainly wasn't hard to look at. Derrick Goodwin was definitely fine as hell. She sat in her car debating on if she should take the $5,000 she had already earned and just run, but she remembered what else was at stake. Destiny couldn't turn her back on her family and the possibility of the woman following through on her deal involving Devon. She knew she had no choice but to keep up whatever the charade she was asked to play. She wished it didn't have to be Derrick, but she did what her heart told her not to do as soon as she heard the beep.

"Hey Derrick, it's Destiny…"

Promises To Keep

7
Bon Appetite

It had been 10 years since he'd lived at home with his parents and yet Derrick still cringed every time he pulled up to his parents' house. He'd tried many times to move his parents to a smaller and more economical place, admittedly for his own selfish reasons, but neither his mother nor father wanted to relocate from their west end Hartford home.

The house was a gift and a curse for Derrick. He appreciated the ability to still come home to a place he'd grown up in. His room was still the same. The landline phone number was still the same, and even his neighbors were still the same. Their neighborhood withstood the evolution of the community surrounding it, so it was good that Derrick still had a place of familiarity after all this time. However, the feeling was bittersweet.

Alongside the childhood memories of this neighborhood, this house also brought the memories of his mother sobbing for nights on end about his father's infidelities. The arguments that ensued due to his dad's late returns from places in close proximity. The countless times his parents yelled and screamed over the phone after his father was asked to leave the house, but continually begged to return. It was difficult for him growing up seeing his mother smile in his face all the while knowing she was hurting. He wanted her so badly to just kick his dad to the curb and finally do something for her and be happy for her, but she never did. She took Derrick's father back every time. Derrick grew resentment towards his mother's weakness, to the point that he couldn't forgive his mother's inability to stand up for herself, especially to his father.

His relationship with his father was iffy. There were moments where he hated his pops for what he did to his mother. Yet, there were also moments when he didn't blame his father for his parents' marital woes - he blamed his mother for allowing it. Ironically, while his father failed miserably at being a husband, he never failed at being a father. He was always there when Derrick needed him or called upon him. Derrick never wanted to be like his father from the standpoint of a lover, but he respected him for the impact he had on his life and aspired to have that kind of impact, be it negative or positive, if he ever had a child. Nevertheless, he still wasn't too fond of family visits.

He pulled up to the house already dreading being there. Derrick knew he needed to stop by and check on his parents more since he didn't have any siblings, but he really didn't enjoy being there. He would have killed to have someone from work call him with a pointless question that he could drag out into something more just so he could leave. He even thought about texting Christy, since Bernice was still on vacation, to have her text him with a false work emergency, but decided against it.

Let me just get this shit over with, he thought to himself.

Derrick could hear laughter coming from the kitchen the moment he opened the front door. It was a bit unusual considering his mom would much rather work in her craft room than watch TV, but it did feel good to hear her laugh.

"Mom!" Derrick screamed from the mini hallway behind the door, but she was still too busy laughing to notice he had walked in the door.

The closer he got to the kitchen, the sooner he recognized the brown Michael Kors handbag that sat on the counter. It was a uniquely designed bag that one would not be likely to forget if they'd seen it, but he certainly wouldn't forget a purse that he purchased last Christmas for one person and one person only. Derrick dropped his keys on the cabinet.

If that bag is here, so is she, Derrick rationalized. He slowly crossed the threshold into the kitchen to find the laughter he heard wasn't of an older woman having a great time baking cookies and watching her favorite show, but the voice of a woman enjoying the company of someone she adored.

"Oh Baby!" his mother said elated after finally seeing Derrick. "Look who stopped by!"

"Derrick."

"Monica," Derrick whispered in return trying to keep his emotions intact. "Quite a surprise to see you here."

"Well I got your message that Miss Ruby wanted me to come by for beef stew. I wasn't able to make it that week, so I asked if I could come by today and . . ."

"I told her she sure could," Ruby interjected. "Monica is always welcomed here and I'm so happy you came too son. We've been in here looking at pictures for so long that I have yet to get the stew started."

Derrick's mom was gleeful that she had some company in the house. She smiled from ear to ear while preparing to season the meat. Derrick found it difficult to hide that he was actually more excited to see Monica than his mother was. It had been several weeks since their last meet and a lot had transpired since then. He needed a few minutes just to catch up, to apologize, and to try to put their friendship back on track. The question was, would Monica let him.

"I was on the brink of horror and embarrassment walking in here. I saw the photo albums on the table and wondered what poor soul was being subjected to mommy's stories."

"Oh hush Derrick," his mother scolded. Derrick laughed, trying to break the ice with Monica, but she

86

wasn't as filled with joy to see him as he was to see her. Derrick was going to have to turn on the charm if he wanted to get to Monica's soft spot. For anyone else, that would have been easy. However, for the woman who knew Derrick better than he knew himself, that was going to be a tall task.

"Miss Ruby, I'm going to go sit on the porch for a little bit until dinner is ready," Monica informed Ruby before rolling her eyes at Derrick.

"Of course my dear," Ruby replied, "in fact, you and Derrick both get outta here and go on the back porch. It's a nice breeze right now too."

"You know what Ma, that's a wonderful idea," Derrick agreed. "Come on Mo, let's go sit on the back porch as my mother instructed."

Monica easily spotted the bullshit in Derrick's voice. She decided to hold her tongue, as to not be disrespectful to Ruby, but the minute she hit that back porch, she had some words for Mr. Goodwin.

"You think you're funny, Derrick?"

"Mo, you've been avoiding me for over a month, what the fuck!"

"And why do you think that is?" Monica questioned with one hand on her hip and her head tilted to her left side.

Derrick paused before responding as he couldn't help but notice how incredible Monica looked. He hadn't laid eyes on her in a while and it almost slipped his mind how easy on the eyes she was. She was in full sorority mode, rocking a bright green head band that matched her pink and green beaded earrings. Her flawless mocha skin looked good in anything, but she was especially sexy to Derrick standing in front of him wearing her high waist jeans that looked painted on, her sorority crop top that hit her midsection just enough to give her navel a peek, and a pair of nude heels that made her 5'6 look more like 5'8. Derrick inched closer to Monica, so close that he could feel her breath and her breast slightly grazing his t-shirt, before finally opening his mouth to speak.

"Mo… I'm sorry."

"Oh shit… here we go with this bullshit."

"No, I mean it Monica," Derrick insisted cutting her off. "I really and truly do apologize to you. For everything. I was a jerk, okay. I wasn't trying to disrespect you. I thought you understood how I felt about relationships. But it was selfish of me not to take your feelings into consideration."

Monica stood there staring at Derrick with her arms folded. Her face had softened, but she wasn't completely sold on Derrick's request for forgiveness. He reached out his hand for hers, and quite naturally she was reluctant to accept it.

"I'm calling for a truce Mo," Derrick continued. "Come on girl, I miss my friend. And I know you miss me too. "

"That's just it Derrick. I don't think I can be friends with you. Being friends with you means seeing you with other women. Hearing about your sexual escapades. Accepting other females asking me to hook them up with you. That's the kind of friend I was. The kind of friend who isn't in love. That's not the kind of friend I am anymore. I shouldn't even be here. You know I love Miss Ruby, but this is all bad. Being here is just all bad."

"You're right. This really isn't a good place to talk. Let's walk up the street to Tisani and grab a drink while we wait for the food."

"That's not what I meant Derrick," Monica countered annoyed.

"Please Mo?"

Monica turned around to head back inside the house when Derrick grabbed her arm, turned her around, and pulled her in close to him, wrapping his arms around her and placing his face near hers.

"Mo… please. Just come get a drink with me. Please?"

Monica dropped her head. She instantly felt fire burning through her bones and the flames were hotter with every moment she spent wrapped in his arms. She just could not say no to this man, no matter how much she knew she should have.

"Fine. One drink. That's it."

Tisani was a small Italian restaurant only two blocks from Derrick's parents' house. Since they were already in the back yard on the back porch, it was really only a block. It was so close, you could see the restaurant awning from where they were standing.

Derrick went inside to tell his mom that he and Monica were walking to get a drink, plus he also needed to grab his cell phone off the counter. He realized he had a couple missed calls and a few text messages, but the only thing he cared about at that moment was getting back in Monica's good graces. Seeing him on his cell phone would trigger a negative assumption and ruin the progress he believed he was making. He wasn't willing to risk it, so he chose to just wait until Monica was not around to check his messages.

They walked to the restaurant in silence. Derrick had so much to say, but thought it to be in better taste to wait until they were in the restaurant. Monica just didn't know what to say. Hell, she barely knew why she had even agreed to come. For the first time in 13 years, it was simply awkward being around each other

When they arrived at Tisani, there were no more seats at the bar, but there were a few tables around it, so Derrick grabbed the table closest to the door. He never sat with his back towards the door and while Monica wasn't too fond of sitting facing away from the entrance, she understood how he felt when it came to that kind of thing, so she retreated to allow Derrick the forward facing seat.

Not two minutes after sitting there, did a blonde bubbly girl come bouncing over to take their order for drinks. She was cheesing extra hard, with her pad and pen in hand.

"Hi, Welcome to Tisani. I'm CeCe your server. What can I get for you to drink to start you off?"

"Glass of merlot for me please," Monica requested.

"Uh… Crown Royal neat please," ordered Derrick.

"Will you two be dining in with us?" CeCe asked.

"Oh no…just drinking," Derrick confirmed.

"Okay great. I'll be right back with those drinks. "

Once the server was gone, Derrick attempted to make conversation.

"So what's new in your life Mo?"

Monica was still guarded. She wasn't at all interested in conversing with Derrick so casually. She wanted him to work for it, earn it, and damn near beg for her conversation. She had to make it tough even if she internally wanted to tell Derrick how miserable she'd been without him. So she sat there.

"Mo... this only works if you try."

"Who said I wanted to try?"

"Seriously Monica? You mean 13 years of friendship down the drain over a misunderstanding?"

"A misunderstanding? Really Derrick? Am I that stupid now?" Monica exclaimed.

"That day you came into the bar, I was having a rough day."

"Oh I'm sure," said Monica rolling her eyes." What, one of your hoes ain't text you back?"

"I'm serious. I was fucked over once again by Rich and more importantly I was upset with myself for hurting you."

"Oh were you now?" Monica questioned sarcastically.

"Yes. I didn't even sleep with anyone that night Mo. I couldn't. I'm not as reckless as you think and that was a total dick move to leave you there after making love to you."

Monica began to sit up a little more in her seat. She was still in disbelief that Derrick was confessing this to her and wasn't totally sold on it, but she needed him to finish.

"You asked me why I fuck you like I love you. Well duh Mo: I do love you and I always have. I have flaws though. Tons of them. You know that. But admittedly I'm selfish. As many women as I've been with, you're not like the others. We got 13 in years Mo. I can't lose you and I can't share you. So what am I to do? "

Monica reached out to grab Derrick's hand just as CeCe was returning to the table with the drinks.

"Thank you," she said to CeCe before turning her attention back to Derrick, this time with a small grin on her face. Her head was struggling to accept his apology, her heart wanted nothing more than to hear Derrick say he was sorry and would never do it again. But she had to be sure an apology was what she was getting. And she had to be clear with Derrick that their friendship had to change.

"Derrick, what exactly are you saying? I know you aren't a relationship type guy. But what exactly do we still have if a relationship is the one thing I want and the one thing you can't give me?"

"Well, I guess what I'm saying is," Derrick began bashfully before noticing a set of red lips and curly hair standing behind Monica in the distance at the hostess stand. He could recognize those lip anywhere. It was Destiny.

She couldn't have come in that restaurant at a worst time. He was just about to tell Monica that he would do his best to keep other woman out of sight and out of mind out of respect for her feelings. But how could he do that now when the woman he'd been lusting after for weeks was standing within in his eye view. For the second time, he was caught with both Monica and Destiny in his presence, and for the second time his heart wanted to choose Destiny, even though Monica seemed like the more sensible choice.

He discretely watched her standing there in a red sleeveless blouse that dipped low in the front and the back. She wore a silver chain that draped her chest with the matching earrings and white low cut shorts that stopped just below the crease of her behind. Derrick was ready for Christmas looking at Destiny in that red and white. She wore open toe clear heels that strapped around her ankles. She resembled an ice-cold mini coke bottle, and Derrick was thirsting for a sip.

He needed to recover his conversation with Monica quickly, as to not bring attention to Destiny's presence. He did not need Monica to see her. He had to bring his focus back to Monica who was two seconds away from turning her head around to see what caused a break in the dialogue.

"You were saying, Derrick?" Monica queued.

"I was saying that umm… yea I sometimes act like an asshole."

"Sometimes?" Monica side eyed.

"Okay … most times."

"Yeah, you do," Monica agreed. "I know I should have been more open to you about what I was truly feeling, but I was in denial honestly."

Monica continued baring her soul to Derrick, but just that fast, Derrick's thoughts were lost in the red lips behind the woman he had just made up with. He didn't lie to Monica about caring for her and even having love for her, but Destiny brought out a feeling in him that he never even realized existed. His heart skipped a beat for a woman whom he'd never even kissed. He was gone off the thought of being inside her when he'd never even seen her naked.

I swear if the pussy is as good as it looks I could be with that woman forever... Derrick thought to himself. Deeper and deeper he fell into his trance of Destiny until unexpectedly his thoughts had left his brain and entered the atmosphere.

"I gotta make you mine. I just have to," Derrick blurted out.

Monica's eyed widened. She couldn't believe her ears. "Are you serious right now?" Monica shouted.

Derrick had become so engrossed in his daydreams of Destiny that he forgot he was talking to Monica.

Oh fuck Derrick!!! He internally screamed at himself. He failed to realize for a split second that he was talking aloud to Monica and he knew he couldn't take it back now. As honest as he prided himself on being with women, he couldn't dare hurt her after he had just so profusely apologized. He had to own it.

Meanwhile, Monica was stunned. *What did he just say?* she kept asking herself. She picked up her glass of wine and began to chug because she was sure she was going to wake up in a moment. But he didn't take it back and he didn't' stutter.

"OMG Derrick… I … I wasn't expecting that!" Monica shouted.

Me neither, Derrick thought to himself.

"You're serious Derrick… no bullshit?" Monica asked for reassurance.

This was his time. If he used the right words and made the right faces with the right winks and right amount of smoothness, he just may have been able to retract. But the way Monica gazed into his eyes while awaiting his answer, he knew if he responded anything other than what she wanted to hear, he would lose her forever. So for the first time in his life, he lied to her.

"What I mean is, I know that I'm not relationship ready, but I'll be more cognizant of your feelings and I'm willing to try because you have to be mine the way you used to be."

He was sure that Monica would be able to see through the bullshit, yet somehow he made her a believer. She stood up and leaned over the table to kiss Derrick.

"It's a start Derrick. I appreciate you at least being willing to try."

Derrick knocked his drink back and gulped hard. Monica waved for the server to return to order another round, feeling celebratory. While she was raising her hand for service, the bulge in Derrick's pants was raising with each glimpse of Destiny. She not even once looked in his direction. She checked her phone a few times, but she was completely oblivious to him being there.

Derrick really needed to talk to her to tell her about his plan for helping her sexual harassment case. They hadn't spoken since she ran out of the office, but he didn't have a contact for her because she left nothing with Christy. He had no way that he knew of to enlighten her on how he could ethically help. This may have been his only chance to let her know, but it was too risky to attempt secretly getting her attention.

Monica decided to order an appetizer even though they were having dinner with Derrick's mom. While she was distracted with her menu, Derrick took the opportunity to write down a little message on his beverage napkin:

Destiny – I can't talk now, but I can help you. Let's meet. Call me ASAP.

He figured if he couldn't get the message to Destiny, the server sure could. His slid the napkin in the checkbook when he placed his credit card inside, so that way once the server saw the napkin with directions written on it for her, she could then deliver the message to Destiny. It was worth a try.

After placing her order, Monica recalled that Derrick mentioned he was having trouble with a case. Monica felt compelled to offer some assistance.

"So what's this court case that's stressing you out?" Monica inquired.

However, Derrick's mind was far from a court case. He was getting harder and harder every second he sat there within eye view of Destiny. He knew it was time to head back to his parents house, but he couldn't leave. Not only would Destiny see him with Monica, but he couldn't walk past a vestibule full of people with a hard-on.

"Come with me," Derrick ordered seizing Monica's hand. He walked swiftly, damn near running, guiding her towards the back of the restaurant where the family bathrooms were located.

"What are you doing?" asked Monica.

But Derrick continued into the bathroom, pulling Monica inside too. He pushed her against the wall, locking the door behind her and linked his lips with hers.

Monica was pleasantly surprised at the unexpected affection; she hadn't been intimate with Derrick in weeks. Her body missed the way he touched her. She matched his passion in his kiss, rubbing her hands across his chest and lifting his shirt to assist in unbuckling his pants.

Derrick turned her around to lean her body over the baby changing station. She arched her back to a customary position and Derrick stood behind her ready to unload.

Derrick used his right hand to unbutton her jeans while using his left hand to explore underneath her crop top. He massaged her breasts softly before lightly licking his fingertips to trace her nipples and heighten her sensation.

The moment he was able to lower her jeans, he moved her blue thong to the side. He was so hard that his manhood was already sticking out of the peephole in his boxers. He raised her hips to meet his waist, and after slipping on a condom, he entered the wetness of Monica.

"Ahhh," Monica squealed at the initial insertion of his rock hard penis.

With a quickened pace, Derrick guided her hips back and forth. Each time he entered her from behind, he could hear the gushing sound from the saturation between her thighs. It gave him the momentum to go harder and faster.

"Yeah, you missed this dick didn't you?"

"Uh…. Uh…" Monica continued to moan. She wanted to answer but couldn't get the words out quick enough.

Derrick continued to swim in Monica's moisture. He leaned his head back, enjoying the tightness closing in on his shaft, but the second he closed his eyes, he began to envision it was Destiny he was sexing. He kept his eyes closed so he wouldn't lose his visualization of Destiny and his imagination began to seize the moment.

He no longer felt Monica's warmth, but instead Derrick felt the heat of a curly haired, red-lipped girl he'd been fiending for since the instant he saw her. The mind games were getting the best of him and Derrick started to feel himself reaching a breaking point sooner than expected. Although he was about to cum in Monica, he was cumming for Destiny.

His breathing was heavy. His heart was beating rapidly. He held on to Monica's waist as he released every ounce he had built up in that moment. He squeezed her ass tightly, so tight that he almost left nail marks in the cheeks of her behind.

"Oh fuck," Derrick screamed. He couldn't remember the last time he had cum so hard. He stood there trying to catch his breath. He opened his eyes to the reality that he was indeed still inside Monica.

She turned her head to smile at him, enjoying the spontaneity of what just occurred, but Derrick couldn't muster the courage to smile back. He just backed away, going to the sink to wipe off and quickly dressing himself back to normal.

When they were done, they exited the bathroom, and Derrick looked towards the hostess stand to see if Destiny was still there. Of course, she had gone. Monica was still trying to get herself together after the unexpected quickie, but she knew they needed to head back to Derrick's mom's house before she started blowing up his phone or even worse, started a search party for her missing child.

Derrick and Monica were halfway out the door before Derrick could hear the waitress CeCe calling his name and running towards him, "Mr. Goodwin! Mr. Goodwin. You forgot your card!"

"Oh shit!" Derrick remembered. He was too busy trying to catch Destiny that he didn't realize he'd never went back to his table to get his debit card or sign the check. With a slight smile, he stepped back inside to receive the receipt book from CeCe.

"Thanks CeCe. I had totally forgotten."

"No worries! It happens," she replied with a wink.

Derrick opened the book to sign his receipt and, to his surprise, was gifted with more than just his debit card.

Promises To Keep

Underneath his receipt was a folded napkin sealed with a set of red lip prints.

8

A Rock & A Hard Place

It was Sunday.

Derrick stood in the middle of an empty Bushnell Park, near the third porta potty, just as the napkin stated. It was chillier than usual outside, and the wind was blowing the smell from the potty right up his nose. He was seriously annoyed with the meeting location, but figured it must have been a reason Destiny wanted to meet there specifically.

After about 10 minutes of waiting with no Destiny in sight, Derrick was ready to leave. The note said she would be there at 8:00 and it was already nearing 8:15. His patience was running thin. While he was eager to provide his assistance and even more eager to see her, Derrick couldn't hide his annoyance with Destiny's lack of punctuality. He hoped nothing was wrong, but he was starting to believe she had just simply decided not to come.

Considering Derrick was usually pretty good at sensing when something wasn't right, and he didn't get that sense in this moment, he concluded she was going to be a no-show and started to feel pretty ridiculous. *Man, what the fuck am I doing out here,* Derrick mumbled to himself.

He repeatedly told himself that he shouldn't be so invested in this girl that he barely knew, but he couldn't shake the notion that meeting Destiny wasn't an accident. As he began to walk towards the street, a shadowy figure approached.

Destiny decided it was time to show face. She had been sitting in a black car parked near the curb the whole time, watching Derrick stand there. She couldn't help but laugh at first. She thought it was kind of cute that he would follow her instructions to a tee.

Standing by the third porta potty Derrick? What on earth for, she giggled. She had no reason for making that specification and thought it was cute how willing Derrick was to do whatever she said. She admired Derrick while she sat there. She had done her research and knew of his bedroom reputation with women. She'd be lying to say that she had not been wanting to discover what flavor of chocolate Mr. Goodwin was from the moment she laid eyes on him, but being in his presence was different from every other mark. Maybe it was because she genuinely had no ill will towards him and didn't want to be in this situation from the start, but it didn't matter. At that point, Destiny snapped back to reality. There was still a task to be done. She exited the car thinking of Devon and the financial gain to come at this end of this. Reminding herself of that made it easier to cope, whether she wanted to do it or not.

Derrick saw someone walking in his direction, and he assumed it was Destiny. The curve of her hips and the curls from the ponytail convinced him it was her. He squinted his eyes a bit to make sure he wasn't imagining her figure as he had often done, but this was no daydream. Destiny was really there. He strolled over to the bench underneath a tree in the park that was far enough from the porta potty to be rid of the smell, but still secluded enough that he and Destiny could talk privately.

"You don't follow directions well," Destiny teased. "This doesn't look like the third porta potty to me."

"You don't tell time well," Derrick countered. "This doesn't look like 8:00 to me."

They shared a quick laugh before simultaneously sitting on a nearby bench. Derrick tilted his body inward a bit to face Destiny, but Destiny continued to sit straight up and forward. A part of her was afraid to look Derrick in his eyes. She'd looked in those eyes before; they were beautiful eyes. The kind that would get you to bear your soul and drop your drawers at the same time. Maybe his ability to persuade people by looking at them was why he was such a good lawyer, and if the rumors were true, an even better lover. Being lost in her thoughts brought a bit of a smile to her face that Derrick couldn't ignore.

"I see those dimples going up and I haven't even told you the good news yet, so what's going on in your head?" Derrick asked.

"Nothing," Destiny lied with a smirk. It was time to do her job.

"So, I got your little message, which is interesting because I had actually called you to set up some time to meet again."

"Did you now? I guess I have to do a better job of answering unknown callers."

"Well, I wanted to apologize. I realized my manners weren't tiptop the last time we saw each other in your office. Storming out, slamming doors, totally inappropriate and that wasn't fair to you."

"Nope… we don't even have to discuss that. In fact, let's forget that ever happened."

"Derrick, you have to let me apologize," Destiny pleaded. She had gotten into character, trying hard to sell her sincerity, and Derrick was buying up all of it.

"You have nothing to apologize for," Derrick assured her.

"Oh, yes I do. I was rude and very temperamental and all you were doing was your job. I could have expressed my frustrations differently. So, please allow me to apologize for that. I'm sorry."

Derrick didn't want or need her apology, but felt this was an opportunity he could use to his advantage. He wanted to see her again without it being related to the case. She wasn't technically a client, so no ethics were being violated, and if anyone asked, she was just a friend he occasionally offered advice to. He was going to take a chance on just going straight for the jugular and hoped that it would work.

"Alright. So here's my deal, I will only accept your apology under two conditions."

"Okay … what are they?"

"Number one, you have to tell me what your favorite food is and number two, you have to let me cook it for you in celebration of the fact that I can help your case."

"Wait, what?"

"You heard me. I have a plan to help you against Jacob West. I can't give you all the details at this exact moment, but you'll have to trust me when I tell you that you can win…."

Destiny was shocked. He wasn't supposed to really know how to help her, let alone help her win. This was spiraling and spiraling fast. But Destiny continued to play the role.

"I know you said you had some news regarding the case, but wow. That's amazing! I don't know what to say."

"Say yes. Yes, you'll let me cook you dinner. Yes, you'll let me help you. I mean I can't technically represent you, that part still stands. But I admit, I was fucked up watching you walk away so angry and not having a solution for you."

"Are you this passionate with all your client's cases?"

"In a way. Then again, you aren't my client."

"Touché."

"What I can say is this," Derrick began, "I'm not usually moved so heavily by someone's situation in the way that I was moved by yours. Second time meeting you and second time seeing you cry. What can I say? Beautiful women crying make me vulnerable."

Derrick lightly placed his hand on her hand as he spoke. Destiny felt a chill shimmer through her body the moment he touched her, which was immediately followed by a punch in her gut that she'd never felt before.

This is so fucked up, Destiny kept saying internally. The gut punch was worse and worse as the conversation went on. Her conscious ate at her like never before and soon, her guilt turned to irritation. She didn't like feeling like a pawn, yet that's exactly what she was.

Derrick's expression was so full of pleasure knowing he had gone above and beyond to make this happen. The more she stared at him, the more she questioned was it all worth it. She wanted to help her brother, but at what cost? How deep into this plot could she go to harm a man who'd been nothing but nice to her, and for what? For reasons still unknown to her. She was done. She was done being a fool and it was time to fess up.

"Derrick, I'm sorry. I can't do this," Destiny said rising to her feet. Her guilty conscious was getting the best of her, but Derrick was not going to let her walk away again. Not without making a full concerted effort to get his dinner date. He stood to his feet and blocked her attempt to leave.

"Nope. No more 'I'm sorry' and no leaving until you accept my terms."

Destiny dropped her head, wanting to escape this scenario as soon as possible.

"Trust me Destiny. I'm not a creep, and I definitely know how to keep my personal life separate from my professional one, but in order to accept these apologies that you insist on giving me, those are the terms. So... will you at least let me cook you dinner?"

Destiny looked in Derrick's face. She could feel herself getting lost in his eyes. She saw him mouthing, "What do you say?", but her ears could hear no volume. The movement of his lips entranced her; she wanted to place her own against them. After asking a second time, Destiny finally responded.

"Sure. Your terms are met."

Without thinking, Derrick reached in to hug Destiny for agreeing. Destiny froze for a second, unable to move her arms or legs. When Derrick sensed her tension, he backed away, instantly upset with himself.

"I wasn't thinking. After everything you've been through at work with West, the last thing you need was for me to touch you like that without your permission. I'm..."

But, before he could complete his thought, Destiny had wrapped her arms around the back of his neck and had locked her lips with his. Their tongues creatively danced with each other and Derrick was stunned at her aggression, but thankful he could finally feel where the lipstick he loved lingered. He pulled Destiny in closer to him, placing one hand on the side of her face, briefly running his fingertips through the sandy brown curls that fell out of her ponytail. When the kiss was over, they stared into each other's eyes briefly, no blinks and no movement, before Destiny broke the silence.

"There is so much you don't know about me."

"I want to get to know everything there is to know about you."

"Derrick, I'm not what you think," Destiny warned. "This ... this isn't what you think."

"I don't understand," Derrick spoke with now both his hands on Destiny's face. "What do you think I think?"

"I'm not some damsel in distress that needs saving. I've done a lot of things, crazy things, but there is something about you. I just... I just don't want to hurt you. There's really something you should know."

Destiny knew she shouldn't have kissed Derrick. She shouldn't have given in to the possibility of falling for him. But she did. And now that she had, the attachment she feared was already creeping up on her. She felt safe with Derrick. She knew she should've just taken the money and run, but that was not an option now.

As she prepared to just spill the beans on the secret scheme to destroy him from the secret person who paid her to make up this ridiculous story about being harassed and filing a lawsuit, she got a text from a cryptic number. She looked down at her phone and nearly gasped aloud at what she read:

Don't even think about it. Say one more word and you can kiss Devon goodbye.

The text had two knife emojis at the end.

Is this son of a bitch watching me? Destiny asked to herself after reading the message. She looked around to see where the spy could be, but saw no one. It was too dark, even in the well-lit Bushnell Park, to see anyone who wasn't standing within feet of her. September in New England brought darkness early in the day, so even though it was only 8:45, it could have easily passed for 2am. That text was a sure sign that any thought she may have had of coming clean with Derrick was a negative. Her eyes began to water and Derrick immediately became concerned.

"Whoa… is everything okay?"

"Yeah, I'm good. I just have to go," Destiny responded.

"What did that message say?"

"It's nothing really. I just have to leave. I'm sorry,"

But Derrick was not making it easy to walk away, still blocking her path.

"Des…"

"'Des'… I have a nickname now? Wow. Interestingly enough, I actually like it," Destiny said trying to laugh through the tears that were running down her face.

Derrick was still clinging on to her hand, but Destiny continued to back away in the same direction in which she appeared, until their hands could no longer touch.

"Promise you'll call me?" Derrick yelled out.

"Dinner date promised," Destiny faintly replied with her voice in the distance.

Derrick was hoping to leave with a feeling of comfort after speaking to her, but now all Derrick felt in this moment was uneasiness. There was something she wasn't saying and he was going to find out what it was.

He watched her walk away then sat back down on the bench to ingest the emotional rollercoaster he found himself riding. Derrick wasn't the fall in love type, but Destiny had a way of erasing Clarice, Melissa, Jackie, and every other woman in his contacts whom he'd regularly visit for sexual favors. But, what scared Derrick the most was her ability to push his feelings for Monica further and further away. No woman had ever done that. He never fathomed anyone could replace Monica in his heart. But he sat on the bench thinking about something he'd never seriously considered with Monica: entering a relationship.

Suddenly, Derrick heard a loud scream of what sounded like female's voice coming from the same direction in which Destiny faded into the darkness. It was pitch black in the Bushnell area; his vision was non-existent outside of the limited spots illuminated by the streetlights. Derrick hurried his steps to see where the noise was coming from, hoping it wasn't Destiny in any trouble. He reached the roundabout where cars usually turned off since the park wasn't open at this hour. There were cars parked on both sides, which was strange considering the street and the park itself was empty, but Derrick continued to feed his curiosity of who may need some help.

Without thinking, or looking, Derrick stepped off the curb between two parked cars. Standing in the middle of the roundabout, Derrick was approached by a black Mercedes Benz with tinted windows undoubtedly doing 80 mph. The high beams blinded him and he raised his hands to block the brightness of the headlights. Within seconds, the vehicle was inches away from Derrick's body with no intent of slowing down.

Derrick began to run, but he wasn't moving fast enough. Beginning to tire, and unable to find a suitable spot to duck out towards the curb, Derrick was certain this was how he was going to die. He could feel the warmth of the car's engine on his legs and soon the fender slightly bumped his calf muscle.

Tripping in the middle of the street, and completely out of breath, Derrick sighed.

It's a fucking wrap, he feared. Breathing heavy, confused and scared, he closed his eyes to accept his fate.

Only it wasn't.

The car stopped abruptly and Derrick turned to find himself staring directly at the Mercedes emblem. The mysterious vehicle began to back away and Derrick started to stand to his feet and catch his breath.

"FUCK IS YOUR PROBLEM!" Derrick shouted at the car angrily.

The back window rolled down and a white envelope was thrown from it, landing in Derrick's direction. The car sped off leaving Derrick, who was now on the curb, frightened and alarmed.

Derrick, still in shock and sweating profusely, was reluctant to walk back into the street, but he had to see what was in the envelope. He swiftly darted back on the curb after picking it up. He headed back to his car, replaying what just happened in his mind, perplexed by the entire situation.

Derrick took a deep breath and opened the packet. One look at its contents and Derrick was red with fury. He crushed the envelope and his hand. *Son of a bitch!*

9
A Hard Bargain

Derrick stormed into his apartment furious. Heading straight for the liquor cabinet, he was sore from being chased down by a random car and even angrier by what he found in that envelope. He needed a glass of Crown to calm his nerves.

Sitting on his leather brown couch with his leg propped, he realized he still had no idea if Destiny was okay. He saw no signs of her being hurt at the scene. In fact, he saw no signs of her at all after she disappeared into the night. The more he sipped, the more he convinced himself that the voice he heard couldn't have been her. Derrick began to believe that there was a mental connection between he and Destiny, and the more he told himself this bond existed, the more he found it easier to relax. "If she was in trouble, I would know. I would feel it," he said aloud before finishing off the glass of Crown.

As he sat, he flashed back to the Benz and forcing his memory to remember the license plate or anything distinctive. Suddenly, he recalled seeing the letter "M" and the number "8." He had a few people who were good with limited resources and knew they would be able to find the car with just the two digits of the plate and a description. It was imperative he was 100% sure that this was who he thought it was. And Derrick was prepared to take his vengeance if the assumption rang true.

Before he could dial up his illegal connect, he noticed he had five missed calls from Monica. He hadn't spoken to her since dinner at his mom's house. He could only imagine how worried she must have been; however, he couldn't call her back just yet. It was necessary for Derrick to have it together when he spoke to her. There could not be holes in the story and there was no way he could actually tell Monica what happened, even if that was the norm. The stack of lies to Monica were piling up, but Derrick could barely think straight for his own well being, let alone trying to persuade someone else that he was ok. Just knowing he was anywhere with Destiny would cause an argument that he was ill prepared to defend.

He watched the notifications from Monica's text messages come through faster than he could delete them. Before meeting Destiny, he would have never let her calls go unanswered or messages go unreturned. She would have been the first person he'd call to tell about what happened tonight and even gone so far as to look to her for answers on how to proceed. Before that kiss Destiny placed on his lips in the park, he would've been asking Monica to come over, using his influential nature to coerce her into giving him a massage for the aching parts touched and untouched by that Benz. He vowed to be more cognizant of Monica's feelings for him and that only affirmed that there was no way he was calling her tonight, even though he needed the company.

He pulled from his pocket the crushed envelope. It was a newspaper clipping of the case MEA loss due to his unethical relationship with the district attorney's witness. This had Rich's name all over it. But ,why?

Unexpectedly, Bernice's number popped up on his phone. Derrick sat up quickly.

This had to be something in the West case, why else would she be calling at this hour? Derrick convinced himself.

"Hey Beautiful," he answered in a raspy voice while trying to clear his throat.

"Hey! You sound horrible though," Bernice replied.

"Yeah, well if you knew what I've been through, you'd understand why."

"Listen, what you do when you're not in between my thighs is not my problem. But given what I'm about to tell you, I sense you'll be back in between my thighs much sooner than later."

Derrick sat all the way up and promptly snapped out of the alcoholic state he was slowly drifting into, "I was already intrigued, but now you have my full attention."

"Can you meet me?"

"Tell me where?"

"The diner on the Berlin Turnpike. Next to the America's Best Motel."

"I'm on the way."

Derrick grabbed his keys and headed toward the door. He limped a little when he walked, but he knew the soreness would wear off. He had no idea what Bernice was going to reveal, but it certainly sounded juicy over the phone, and quite frankly, so did Bernice. He knew what her promised her if she continued to bring him internal information on the West case, but the way he desired attention, coupled with the glasses of Crown, Derrick would have taken Bernice without the incentive.

The moment he opened the door, Derrick spotted a white card on the ground near the threshold. He bent down to pick it up to find the only ten digits he'd ever care to see – Destiny's phone number! *She must have slid it in my pocket while we kissed.* Derrick assumed. He didn't know how it got there or when he dropped it, and honestly, he didn't care. His first instinct was to call and make sure she was ok, but on second thought, he decided to handle this business with Bernice first.

Upon arrival at the diner, Derrick checked out the surroundings of the parking lot and the neighboring businesses. The Berlin Turnpike was the perfect place for someone to trail or follow, and considering the events that took place earlier that night, he wasn't too trusting anymore. . He watched his back as if he was Jerry Ferreira on an episode of *Power,* flinching at the possibility that Ghost could kill him. Thing is, he never had any "Ghost" like clients, and until tonight, there was never a reason for anyone to attempt to threaten his life. Anything could happen for any reason and he wanted to be prepared.

Many people didn't know this about Derrick, but he was a skilled marksman. His father used to take him to the gun range as child, and he often still made trips to the range in his spare time. Derrick always aspired to be a litigator, but considered law enforcement as a second option in case law school didn't work out. For protection, he kept a Glock 17 in his car at all times, registered of course. He hoped he'd never need to use it, but he treated his pistol like a condom - he'd rather have it and not need it, than to need it and not have it.

Once he saw the lot was clear, he went inside where he found Bernice sitting on the backside of the bar closest to the wall. He could tell by her seat selection she was trying to be discreet, which he appreciated. Both he and Bernice had a lot on the line with what they were doing. He was asking her to put her career in jeopardy by retrieving this information for him illegally, and while Bernice was attractive, smart, funny, and hella sexy, she was also very thorough. It would eat Derrick alive if something happened to Bernice or worse, if Rich retaliated against her by firing her or ruining her reputation that would hinder her from finding another quality firm to work for. He thought about the consequences often if this plan didn't work, which was why he was hell bent on making sure that it did.

"What's with that walk?" Bernice questioned.

"Tripped and fell earlier. Might have pulled a hamstring," Derrick answered.

"Never took you for the clumsy type," Bernice side eyed, "are you sure you're okay?"

"Usually when I trip and fall it's into something with a bit more cushion than a concrete pavement. But, nothing a hot bath and maybe a massage won't cure."

Bernice squinted her eyes. She knew exactly what Derrick was alluding to and her panties moistened at the thought of Derrick tripping and falling in her hotspot. She was sure that's what awaited her after she shared what she discovered in the West case.

"You just might be in luck sir, especially after this."

Bernice reached into her bag and pulled out a manila folder labeled Davis vs. West. Bernice had managed to snag the entire case file. Derrick was elated.

"Bernice you're a fucking truth! I don't even want to know how you did it."

"Good, because I wasn't going to tell you, and I definitely plan to put it back before someone notices it's missing, but peep who the main plaintiff is."

Derrick skimmed the contents of the folder, coming across a picture that struck him as oddly familiar.

"This face is familiar to me but I can't place why I recognize it. Glenda Davis?"

"That's because the last time you saw that face, it had a mustache and a beard and went by the name Glenn Davison."

'HOLY SHIT! This is Glenn? Former accounting executive Glenn who McEnroe fired a few years back!"

"Yup!" Bernice confirmed. "After he left MEA, he started working for Jacob West, but he'd never applied as a man, only as a woman. And that's not even the kicker."

"Jacob West has a sexual harassment suit filed against him from a transsexual, how can this get any better?" Derrick chuckled.

"Oh, it does. Davis went to Columbia. You know who else went to Columbia?"

"Fucking Rich McEnroe!" Derrick hollered with the widest of eyes.

"Roommates, Derrick. They were fucking college roommates. And when I say fucking, I mean it as literal as the word gets. "

Derrick couldn't have planned this any more perfect. His mouth flew open and there was no way to shut it with the intel he just received. The more he thought about it, the more it began to make so much sense as to why Rich would never want him lead counsel on this case.

West was a high profile client and Derrick's name rang bells since the St. James case. They were not going to want this public. It would be humiliating for West and even more so for Rich, considering the conflict of interest.

"But look Derrick, there's more. Like three other women are in on this lawsuit. All of which are young, white, and blonde. This reeks of a #MeToo case," Bernice continued.

"And if that happened, the media would be all over this. But wait, are these the only four people currently involved in this lawsuit?"

"So far, yes," Bernice responded.

Derrick knew exactly how he was going to help Destiny and even more so, how he was going to get Rich off his high horse, especially if his suspicion is confirmed about his involvement in the car attack.

Derrick was very please with the information Bernice gave, and also very horny. He looked at Bernice, licking his lips, "So about that massage for this leg. If I can manage to limp over to the America's Best, can you help me work out the soreness?"

Until he could have Destiny the way he wanted her, he was to be happy to settle for Bernice. She came through on her end of the deal and now it was time for him to come through on his.

Bernice had been waiting to hear that all night. "You ain't said nothing but a word," she replied.

Derrick took a few screenshots of some key information from the folder and handed it back to Bernice who secured it in her bag. Derrick made sure that folder was exactly the same as it was when Bernice took it. Nothing could be out of order. His plan was flowing smoothly and he'd come too far to see it fail now due to a slip up on his part. Before he'd move on to phase two, he'd have to wait for Bernice to return the folder.

Meanwhile, Bernice had already reserved a room on the second floor in the motel next door to the diner. She anticipated on ending her night with a sweetness that only Derrick could provide. He couldn't close the door fast enough before Bernice was ripping his jacket off and clawing her way to his belt buckle. With each kiss that Bernice placed on his neck and check, Derrick could feel his manhood expanding. Bernice's arousal tripled with each bulge she felt, as she rubbed his pants to further his expansion. It had been too long since she last had a piece of Derrick Goodwin and she was ready to feed her craving. Derrick's mind was in a million places, but his body was certainly attentive to what was occurring in room 201.

It wasn't long before Bernice had dropped to her knees, yearning to be face to face with Derrick's rock hard penis. Unbuckling his pants, she lightly eased down the zipper of his jeans. She glanced up to see Derrick's head beginning to lean back against the wall. She lowered his pants to mid-thigh, smiling at the sight of his excitement in front of her. She'd never wanted to put her mouth on a man as much as she did in that moment.

Derrick eagerly wanted to enjoy Bernice's oral pleasures, but his body betrayed his mind. The pain from his leg was hard to ignore, and weakness would soon take over. As much as he appreciated the view of Bernice kneeling in front of him, he motioned to move their foreplay to a chair located near the door.

Once Derrick was seated, Bernice continued her quest to taste all Derrick had to offer. She lowered his pants even further, removing them completely from his body, and tossed them behind her. She spread his knees wider, as Derrick shifted himself forward just enough to give her the complete access she needed to inhale his massiveness.

"You look real comfy," Derrick said.

"I am," Bernice smirked.

She unbuttoned her shirt, giving Derrick another look at her well-adjusted breasts that sat perfectly in the blue and gold-laced bra she was wearing. Bernice's skin glowed against the lamp in the room. The sight of her made Derrick hard enough to break down a door without his hands or his feet.

Bernice moved in closer to him, gliding her melons against Derrick's shaft, burying it in the warm creases of her chest, and licking the tip with every upward motion. he gave a small gasp of delight with each tickle from her tongue. With the final upward thrust, she placed her lips over the sticky flesh of his head. The wetness of her mouth felt like heaven. Derrick groaned in the back of his throat until Bernice decided to pick up the pace.

She opened her mouth wider, deep throating his deliciousness. Her gag reflexes were second to none, and Derrick reached for the back of her head as she glided her mouth up and down on his wood. She slid her tongue down to his base, using her other hand to lightly stroke his balls. Derrick's groans turned into pants, which eventually turned into moans, indicating he was nearing his climax.

Bobbing her head faster, Bernice took in all of Derrick, allowing her tongue to move languidly against the underside of his smooth rock cock. Cupping his balls and twisting her head to ensure his entire shaft was covered in her saliva, Bernice found her rhythm. She felt Derrick's body pulsating and knew he was on the brink of release. He motioned for her to move away, warning her of his oncoming orgasm, but Bernice had no intention of loosening her oral grip of Derrick.

Completely stiff, Derrick's leg muscles tightened around Bernice's sides. Grasping for air and reaching for the arms of the chair, Derrick could no longer hold on and began to explode. Bernice sucked harder as he came, swallowing every ounce that streamed from Derrick, not wanting to waste a single drop. Derrick couldn't remember the last time he'd received some head that fire that made him cum that hard.

Once he was done, Bernice proceeded to button her shirt and stand to her feet, looking for a mirror to adjust her clothes.

"Whoa... we're not done. I haven't had my turn with you," Derrick said.

"Oh yeah, we're done. You go home and nurse that leg. Your debt is paid."

"I feel used," Derrick teased. "Took my manhood and putting me out."

Bernice laughed, "I have to get this file back so I don't have time to mess around with you any longer."

"Damn... and I can't make you cum at least once?"

Bernice grabbed her jacket and her bag after reapplying her lipstick before replying to Derrick.

"No need to make me cum once, when you've already made me cum twice."

She winked at Derrick, opened the door, and scurried down the stairs to her car. She didn't even leave her tropical/coconut scent for Derrick to savor. She got in her car, knowing Derrick was still standing at the top of that motel balcony confused on what just happened. She smiled.

One for Bernice, zero for Derrick.

***

The table was filled with lawyers, doctors, accountants, and other well to do professionals who customarily crowded Casa Mia for evening drinks. The conversations almost always started with how intellectually challenged their staff and employees were, then shifted to how putting up with them is all worth it due to the enormous amount of revenue they generated from the backs of these "dimwits", and normally ended with some trip that one or more of them would be taking in the next week or so with the money they collected.

To the naked eye, one would think that this engaged Rich but, in all actuality, he found these events to be filled with meaningless dialogue that he despised and he wished he didn't have to pretend to enjoy them.

Truthfully, he only suffered through these dinners to keep up appearances. MEA had an extensive list of affluent clients and it was part of Rich's job to ensure those clients remained happy, not only with their legal representation, but their social representation as well.

It was one of the reasons that Rich cringed at the thought of doing pro-bono services, even though he had to under the ABA. He didn't want MEA to ever acquire a reputation of being, for lack of a better term, affordable. He wanted to remain the crème de la crème in the New England power structure of attorneys, and that meant he had to continue to bore himself to death at dreadful dinner parties and casual engagements.

Rich needed an escape. He ran through scenarios in his head, trying to find the one that would be fitting enough for an early exit but not too extreme that would call for questions later. Just as he thought he'd come up with a perfect story, he felt his phone vibrate in his jacket pocket. He looked at the screen, unable to recognize the number, and thought twice about answering, but decided that it may be the out he was searching for.

"Excuse me. I have to take this, sorry," Rich announced before pushing away from the table to take his call. Pretending to smile as he walked through the crowd towards the bar area heading to the bathrooms, Rich curiously questioned the identity of the caller.

"I don't know this number, so who is this and speak quickly."

"Trust me, I don't want to make this conversation any longer than it needs to be."

"Goodwin? What the hell is your problem man? Why are you calling me from this random number?" Rich inquired.

"Would you have answered on the first ring had I called from my own line?" Derrick asked, refusing to disclose that he was actually calling from his Google Voice number.

"Usually no, but under the circumstances, I may have made an exception. What do you want Goodwin?"

"Listen Rich, I have no desire to be friends with you. I barely have a desire to work with you, yet here I am once again ready to offer you a chance to save your career and your firm."

"Have you lost your fucking mind?" Rich replied with a smirk on his face. "YOU save MY career and MY firm? In what world would I ever need you to save me? And save me from what? I'm in no danger and even if I was, you would be the last person I would call to my aid."

It took Derrick an insane amount of patience to sit through the useless soliloquy that Rich insisted on giving; however, his patience was running thin. He decided it was time to cut the bullshit and get right to the nature of things. As Rich paced back and forth in the small hallway past the bar, he was sure he was alone until he wasn't.

Out of nowhere a large hand grabbed Rich by the back of his sport coat and aggressively pushed him into the men's restroom. Rich was so frightened he almost peed his pants.

"You are one self-centered bastard," Derrick snarled with his hand in Rich's chest, gripping his shirt tightly as he hemmed Rich against the back of the bathroom door and his left fist balled to his side.

"What the hell are you doing here?"

"Well, I was in the neighborhood," Derrick responded.

"More like a stalker to me, now let me go Goodwin or I will make you regret this. You still work for me. And you are still on probation under the care of MY office. So let me go," Rich growled.

"Just like the white man wanting to throw up shit in your face. And I know that was you that tried to run me over. You want to take me out, try harder next time," Derrick said angrily.

"What? What the hell are you talking about, I've been here all night," Rich exclaimed.

"Then one of your cronies I'm sure," Derrick yelled back more aggressively.

"I swear to you, it wasn't me!"

Derrick had a mind to just punch Rich in the face for the hell of it. But he knew he had to learn to control his emotions when it came to Rich, and he also needed to remember the bigger picture - Destiny.

The more he stared at Rich, the more he sensed the truth. It wasn't him. Derrick slightly eased up his grip, but he was still very much in Rich's face. He was still in too much pain from the earlier events to really go blow to blow with Rich, but he would if it came down to it. However, as much shit as Rich talked, he was very much afraid of the man that stood before him.

"Just tell me what it is that you want Goodwin."

"I want the West case."

"No. I cannot, no, I WILL not put you on that case. And if you desire to beat me up or whatever it is you

127

people do get your way, so be it. I'll have your license forever and you'll never practice law again."

Something clicked in Derrick's head. He should have known better than to try and muscle a guy like Rich, so he slowly began to back away. He watched Rich grow a little taller, thinking he had the upper hand, but Derrick stood there in a place of enjoyment knowing that he was about to rip all smugness right off of his boss' pale face.

"Glad you've come to your senses," Rich said.

"And it's too bad you didn't come to yours," Derrick rebutted. "You see, your little friend Jacob West aside from being a little too friendly with Glenda, or shall I say your ex Glenn, forgot that there was one additional victim whose name never made it onto the report. This particular victim is ready to testify right now before a judge and spill all the beans on West and his entire filthy operation and history of sexual assault.

"Quite honestly, this victim would rather move on with her life. She knows the repercussions of speaking out. She'll potentially lose her job and her benefits. West's believers will slander her name and she'll forever live with the disgust of what happened in a public light. And while that would be hard, she's still willing. Why you ask? Because her testimony would destroy West."

"How the hell do you know anything about this case? Who have you been talking to? And if I were to say you're right about the parameters of the case, you expect me to believe you or this little story you tell about a fourth victim?"

"Nope," Derrick spoke sternly. "I don't. Which is why I'm advising her to file a civil lawsuit once this little charade you're going through is over. Sure you'll get West off. But, she won't come to you with her name. You won't be able to persuade her like the other three victims. She's solidly saying 'fuck you'."

Rich's eyes were bugged. His breathing had slightly increased, and he knew that Derrick was telling the truth. Rich was ill prepared for a fourth victim of whom he had no knowledge and no intel. He wasn't exactly sure who to point fingers at in terms of being the mole that leaked the info to Derrick, but he knew Derrick was too smart to come to him with this if it wasn't true. Rich felt a kick in the pit of his stomach, because this was the part where some kind of negotiation was about to happen, and the last thing he wanted to do was give in to Derrick Goodwin, yet again on a case that could catapult his career, and destroy his in the process. But he had no choice.

"So what needs to happen to keep her from talking?" Rich asked loathing the thought of needing Derrick once again to keep his firm's reputation intact.

"Make me lead counsel. She trusts me. She trusts my advice. Make me lead counsel on the case, I'll follow through with the plan you have in place for the other three victims, and I'll have this one settle out of court for $1M, no less."

"Are you out of your mind!" Rich yelled.

"And what do you think she'll sue him for, pennies? Fuck no. It will be more MUCH more. But hey, this is now your problem. I tried to be a decent human being. You would rather be a prick. So, you've got it."

Derrick rolled his eyes at Rich and prepared to push him away from the door so that he could exit when Rich finally conceded.

"Fine," Rich spoke softly, looking down at the ground with his hands on his hip. "You're now lead counsel. Make this shit go away."

Derrick turned to walk out the door and nodded his head to affirm the agreement they just made.

10
Victory Formation

Destiny sat on the edge of her bed with her phone in her hand debating to herself whether or not she should call or text Derrick. This gig was getting to her. She wasn't in control and because of that, she was unsure of what the next move was. She was constantly under the microscope and for what? For Derrick?

In the grand scheme of things, she could see why. He was incredibly handsome and he had a way of making her feel unlike anyone else ever had. They didn't have a ton of time in each other's presence, but each time made her heart and her body feel more and more inclined to be in his presence again and again. But what could he have possibly done to these people wanting to harm him that would make them go so far as to pretend to run him over. She watched the events unfold from the back of the truck in a nearby parking lot and was at a loss for words.

She felt herself starting to slip into a protective trance the moment she received those text messages threatening harm to Derrick. As much as she was about her money, she was not about getting it at the expense of his life. She wasn't about getting it at the expense of any of it at this point. Destiny was losing herself. The badassery was gone. She no longer wanted to be scared that someone was watching her or calculating her every move.

Fuck it, she thought to herself. *It's time to get back to me.*

She got off her couch and went to her room to take off her leggings and throw on some jeans under the black crop top she was wearing. She was done with this and wanted to let whoever was running things know face to face that she would no longer play this game at the expense of someone's life anymore. She would find another way to help her brother, but this was done.

The moment she got to her room, her phone began to ring. She didn't readily recognize the number and she assumed it was exactly who she wanted to speak to.

Who else would be calling me from a number I don't know? she asked herself and picked up the phone with the same assurance.

"You know, this time I'm glad you called, because I have a few words for you," Destiny said harshly.

"I hope those words are 'I'm okay.'"

"Derrick?"

She did not expect to hear his voice on the other end of the line, but admittedly she was delighted to hear it. "I see you found my package I left for you?"

"I did," Derrick answered, "but are YOU ok? You disappeared out of nowhere. I heard a woman scream from the same area, and I was worried sick that something had happened to you."

Destiny sighed, "I'm sorry I frightened you. It wasn't me screaming, but I guess I could have let you know I made it home safely."

"Don't apologize. You're fine and now I'm fine. In fact, I'm better than fine because I have news that's going to knock your socks off."

"Oh really? Well now, I'm intrigued."

"You've gotta let me tell you in person. Where can we meet?"

"Here," Destiny replied. The words came out so fast, she didn't even realize how quickly she had responded.

"Are you sure?" Derrick asked. "I don't want to intrude on your personal space." But the more Destiny listened to the bass in his voice, she wanted nothing more than for him to intrude on her personal space.

"It's totally fine. I didn't have any plans. I'll text you the address."

"Text this number. It's my Google number."

"Alright...I guess I'll see you in a few."

"Looking forward to it."

Destiny hung up the phone more anxious than she was when she was building up the courage to get out of this mess. She wasn't at all anticipating hearing Derrick's voice on the other end of the phone and yet the thought of him heading to her apartment aroused her in a way she didn't expect. She didn't even think he would notice that she slipped her number in his pocket. But whom did she think she was fooling, Derrick didn't miss anything.

She looked around her apartment and made sure there was nothing out of place. She didn't keep a dirty house, but she wasn't above having a pizza box or a random pair of draws somewhere they didn't belong. Before she knew it, she got a text from Derrick alerting her he was coming off of Asylum Ave. He was less than five minutes away from her place. Her heart raced.

"Get it together, D," she said aloud to herself. "You act like ya'll have never been alone together before." But the reality was, they hadn't. His colleagues were around when they met in the office and his enemies watched when they were in the park. The truth was, this was indeed going to be their first time alone with nothing but each other.

Destiny didn't get a chance to touch up her hair or even put any gloss on her lips before there was a buzz at her door. She took a deep breath, understanding this was the moment of truth, and opened the door to find Derrick standing there. Destiny was unable to find the words to break the silence that stood between them. She wasn't sure why she had all the sudden become more nervous than usual, but it was something about Derrick that encapsulated her confidence.

"Are you going to invite me in or are we going to chat out here?" Derrick said jokingly.

"Oh shit… yes, please come inside."

It was inching closer to 12:45a and somehow Destiny seemed even more beautiful in her home dressed down with just leggings and a crop top than she did when he was with her earlier that evening in the park. Her hair was all over her head, but the free flowing curls worked for her. Her black tube socks made Derrick giggle a little, as they reminded him of something a young cheerleader would wear. His thoughts begin to get the best of him as he started to chuckle visibly.

"What's so funny?"

"It's nothing," he lied.

"Liar," Destiny teased. "I want to laugh, come on tell me."

"Well if you must know, you kind of remind me of a little cheerleader with those tube socks and your curly hair. All you need are some pom poms and some pumpkin seeds," Derrick confessed.

"Shut up," Destiny said rolling her eyes, playfully hitting Derrick on the shoulder. He stepped backwards to avoid her and forgot that his leg was not at full strength. He stumbled lightly.

"Whoa, Derrick. Are you okay? What happened to your leg?" Destiny remembered the events from the park were causing the pain. She couldn't let on that she knew why he was hurting, but she felt terrible. As he explained the events after her departure, she had made up in her mind that she had to end this.

"Enough about this. I didn't come over here to talk about me. I came over here to tell you about how you're going to be a million dollars richer come Monday morning."

"Come again? "Destiny asked puzzled. "What do you mean a million dollars?"

"I told you I was going to find a way to help you win your case. I figured out who the plaintiff is on the West case. When you told me that your complaint had not been added to the case, I used it as leverage. My boss had no idea a fourth victim was out there and when he found out, he was shook!"

"Wait a minute, you told someone about me?"

"Well not exactly. He knows a fourth victim exists, but I didn't tell him your name and I may have over exaggerated your case a little bit and the extent you would be willing to go to nail West, but I knew if Rich thought there was no way out, he'd conform. And he did."

Destiny was shocked. She didn't know what to say or how to feel. This man literally risked his life and career to help her for a phony case. How was she supposed to celebrate that? She plopped down on her couch staring at Derrick. "Wow Derrick… that's, that's amazing news."

"Don't thank me yet. There is this one small part. I know you want to fry this guy. He deserves to be fried for what he did to you and those other women, but in order to get this deal you have to be willing to settle out of court and sign an NDA saying…"

"Hold on," Destiny said cutting off Derrick. "I have to sign an NDA?"

"I know it stinks. It'll require that you won't speak on this matter again. But I have another plan in motion to fry Jacob West, so trust me when I say he won't be getting off. But this is a great deal for you. You'll walk away with $1M and that should be more than enough to get you started with you own accounting firm. You won't need West or anyone else."

Destiny was still trying to process what she was just told. It wasn't the details of the NDA that worried her, it was the notion of signing anything that had her scared shitless. The moment she walked into that room, Jacob West or any of his representatives would not recognize her. She wasn't an employee. The jig would be up. She wanted to get out of this debacle on her own terms, not by getting caught on being messy. At the same time, maybe she could disguise herself. It was a million dollars. And that would be more than enough to help her brother and get outta dodge. She was unsure of what to do and needed to talk to The Boss. In that moment, Destiny did the only thing she could do. She agreed.

"Sure Derrick. I'll come in first thing Monday morning and sign the paperwork." Destiny cracked the fakest smile and stood up from the couch. "Let's celebrate."

She hurried to the kitchen to grab a bottle of chardonnay. She cracked it open and gulped a glass to take the edge off before pouring another glass for her and a fresh glass for Derrick. She decided in the kitchen she was going to go for what she knew. For what she always did.

She would get her coins and get on about her business. She figured she might as well savor this moment with Derrick because she was sure it would be her last one.

"Here you go. Hope you like Chardonnay."

"I love Chardonnay," Derrick affirmed.

"Thank you so much for doing this Derrick. I truly don't know how to thank you."

"There's no need to thank me. I'm a man of my word, and I made a promise to help you. I'm just glad I could honor that."

Destiny smiled and raised her glass, "A toast to victory."

"Hear, hear."

The two sipped their wine after their cheers and the electricity in the room seemed to spark more with each sip. The two killed another bottle of chardonnay and talked for another 30 minutes before Derrick realized it was almost 1:30am. He could feel himself losing his ability to be a gentleman and didn't want to come off disrespectful.

"I should be getting out of here. It's getting late and I don't want to keep you up."

Destiny placed her finger over Derrick's lips to shush him. "You worry too much about the wrong things," Destiny replied. "How about you just enjoy the night and see where it takes us."

Derrick didn't wait and took matters into his own hands. He grabbed Destiny's hand while her finger was still on his lips and began to sensually slide her finger in his mouth. Each stroke of Derrick's tongue on her finger tingled Destiny in her center space. Derrick slowly transitioned from a suck of her finger to a kiss on the palm of her hand and then moved his way down her arm until he had pulled her close enough to him to taste her lips.

He delicately sucked her bottom lip before softly kissing the top one. With each kiss, Destiny's tingles intensified until she was unable to mask how much she wanted to indulge in the likes of Derrick Goodwin. She needed this. Hell, she'd earned it in her mind. They both did after all they had been through in the last eight hours.

Destiny gradually laid back on the couch with Derrick settling over her. He gently rubbed her exposed tummy all the while placing tender kisses on her neck. Destiny guided his hands towards her chest, signaling for Derrick to caress the bare breasts that lie under her crop top. He lightly lifted her shirt and mouthed each nipple, watching them stiffen with each touch.

Derrick wanted to ensure this moment with Destiny wouldn't be limited by the small space of the couch. He needed to give her all of him. He picked her up and carried her to her bedroom. The king size bed provided all the space Derrick needed.

As they continued to passionately embrace each other, Destiny paused and began to slide off her leggings. Derrick stopped to observe the striking beauty of the naked woman that lay before him. His manhood hardened by the second, yet he fought the desire to enter her. He wanted to taste every bit of her first.

Spreading her legs far enough apart for him to slither his face inside her thighs, he allowed his tongue to take over. Derrick was a master at giving head and Destiny quivered with each stroke. He could feel her body pulsating as he sped up his pace. Her moans informed Derrick she was reaching her climax and he didn't plan to stop until a creamy puddle of wetness had moistened every inch of his face.

"Oh God, Derrick. I'm gonna cum. I'm gonna cum," Destiny cried out, clinging on to the back of Derrick's neck. She trembled as she erupted, leaving a pool of her juices in the spot where she lay. But that wasn't enough for Derrick. He could no longer resist the urge to enter her. He placed the condom on his rock hard erection and slipped into the dampness of her womanhood. His slow thrusts felt like heaven to Destiny. He was just the right size and had the right amount of thickness to touch her insides completely.

Settling over her with one hand behind her head, he penetrated her steadily. Her faces were those of pain and pleasure. Her box was warm and it took so much concentration from Derrick not to bust instantly. But minute after minute he pounded her very core. Her screams became his cheers. Her tremors became his cues that she was getting closer and closer to reaching another orgasm, until finally he was unable to stop the eruption that flowed from his staff.

The sweat that dripped between them was evidence of the fire and passion that they shared.

Neither of them could speak.

Both of them entirely satisfied.

140

And with just one glance, they knew their night had just begun.

Promises To Keep

11
Unexpected News

Monday's weren't usually Derrick's favorite day of the week, yet this Monday was going to be the best he'd had in a while. Bernice was back in the office from vacation so he knew his schedule would be on point and Rich had already set up a meeting with the partners to inform them he would be taking over as lead counsel on the West case. But more importantly, Destiny would be coming by around noon to sign the non-disclosure agreement and get the settlement rolling.

Derrick stared at his clock as he counted down the minutes until he would see Destiny again. The two of them made love over and over again, and she was all he could think of.

He continued to avoid Monica. He just wasn't sure what he could say or how he could say to her that he was just not in the right headspace to attempt a relationship with her anymore. Especially not after last night; not after being with Destiny.

Derrick occupied his time with a few phone calls and some emails, but the moment the clock struck 11:00, his excitement and anticipation grew. Before he could finish his last email for the morning, he received an instant message from Bernice to his computer: I couldn't stop her.

Derrick looked up to see Monica walking right to his office with two bags from Panera Bread.

"Hey my love! I've missed you," Monica exclaimed happily as she walked right over to Derrick and kissed him hello. She placed the Panera bags on the chair and began to empty its contents on Derrick's desk.

"I have been trying to reach you all weekend. I figured it had to be a case that has you all riled up and ignoring everyone and everything, which means knowing you, you haven't eaten properly in days. So I figured I'd stop by and bring you some grub. I got your fav: broccoli and cheddar bread bowl and a turkey sandwich."

Derrick was in too good a mood to care that Monica bogarted her way into his office and was glad that she assumed his absence was work related. As an attorney, she knew how easy it was for a case to consume you. This was a great segue to tell Monica about being lead counsel.

"Thanks so much for thinking of me, you're right. I have been consumed with a case, but it's paying off. Today as a matter of fact!" Derrick bragged.

"Oh, really?" Monica intriguingly responded, "How's that?"

"Well, remember that case I was having some trouble with?"

"Yeah, the one you wanted my help on."

"Yes! Well, turns out no help is needed. "

Derrick gave her the rundown on how he was able to help Destiny and what his plan was moving forward in the Jacob West case.

"So you see, this is why I don't have time for lunch because in about 30 mins, Destiny is going to walk in that door, sign the NDA, walk out a million dollars richer and I am going to be lead counsel on the biggest case this firm has seen since the St. James case. Mo, this day can't get any better. "

Monica stared at Derrick. She was happy to see Derrick excited about his opportunity to advance, but she wasn't fooled by Destiny. She knew Destiny was the girl from the bar, even if Derrick never said so. She knew that girl. She never forgot a face.

"Derrick, you deserve everything coming to you and more," Monica assured Derrick smiling.

"Thanks Mo." He hugged Monica, gave her a kiss on the cheek, and headed out the office up to the boardroom.

Monica stood there in the office with her 3 piece navy blue and gold suit on waving back to Derrick as he prepared to enter the elevator. The moment he was out of sight, she looked around his desk to see what she could find about Destiny's case. She tried to hurry, not wanting to be caught, especially by Bernice. But soon, she saw what she needed. She pulled out her phone to take a pic of the notes and headed out the door, dialing someone from her contacts.

"Hey Jay, it's Monica Lawrence. I need you to run a name for me and tell me what you find…"

…

Derrick was pacing outside the boardroom. It was close to 11:56 and there was no sign of Destiny. He called her over and over again and there was nothing. The phone actually rang, which meant it wasn't dead and it wasn't being sent to voicemail. Either she had the ringer off or she was watching the phone ring. He couldn't understand why either would be happening right now. They had a clear understanding of what today meant. Destiny had no idea that his position as lead counsel was on the line, and while he was also concerned that she was nowhere to be found, this meant everything to him too.

He glanced at his watch once more, viewing the hand change to 11:59. Derrick had walked into the boardroom; livid with every step he took.

"Mr. Goodwin, it's noon as we agreed. Where is your client?" Rich asked.

"I'm sure she's running just a little bit behind. You know how traffic is in Downtown Hartford for the lunch rush," Derrick worriedly uttered.

"Mr. Goodwin, if you're client isn't here in five minutes…"

"Just give her a minute Rich. She'll be here."

While the other associates in the room shared the same look of concern as Derrick, Rich instead had a growing grin. The more frustrated Derrick became, the more satisfied Rich became. Each passing minute gave Rich more and more leeway to dead this agreement. As soon as 12:05 hit, Rich seized the moment.

"Gentlemen, I deeply apologize for the waste of your time. I called this meeting under the notion that Derrick would be bringing us at least a partial resolution to the West case. But of course, that was all talk and no bite."

"You know I didn't make this up Rich!" Derrick shouted.

"Then where is this key witness who'll 'destroy' our case? Not here. And I can't help but wonder did she ever exist and if this just a ploy to get your way? Well if it was, it didn't work. And this further proves why you are not ready to be involved in this case. Let alone lead counsel. Gentlemen, we're dismissed."

Rich glared at Derrick devilishly. He knew he'd won the moment and had taken back control of the dynamic between them. Derrick knew it too. But he wasn't mad at not being lead counsel. He wasn't even mad at Rich's bold attempt to embarrass him. He was hurt that Destiny would stand him up after promising to be there. After everything he'd done and been through to make this happen for her, he didn't understand why she'd say she'd come and not show up, call, or text. Last time he assumed something was wrong, she was sitting at home unharmed on her couch. Far be it for him to assume the worse now. He took a deep breath, stood up, and began to walk back to his desk.

As he slowly trudged towards the elevator, his phone rang. It was Monica.

"Yes, Mo."

"Derrick...I knew your girl was bogus. "

"What are you talking about Monica?"

"Your girl Destiny. She isn't employed by Jacob West and Co. She's never worked there. Her name is Destiny Turner, and she's as fake as a $3 bill. Check your email, sending it now."

Derrick didn't even say goodbye. He hung up the phone and rushed back to his office, deciding to take the stairs. Running down the 4 flights, he thought back to each encounter, replaying how he didn't once ever do his due diligence as an attorney. He didn't once check her story out. He never Googled her, never looked her up on Jacob West's website, nothing. He took her at her word and believed everything she said because she said it.

He brushed past Bernice and went into his office, heading straight for his computer. He opened his email to find the one thing he was not ready to believe or accept. Monica was right. Destiny was a fraud.

12
Background Check

Derrick sat in his car and called Destiny again and again. He needed to know from her own mouth why she would lie to him. Why would she allow him to go so far? Was it all a scam? *No it couldn't be. She felt something for me, I know she did.* Derrick tried to convince himself.

He felt ridiculous and played. He had never allowed himself to become vulnerable at the hands of a woman before and couldn't believe how easily he let it happen. He was totally against relationships and yet here he was, feeling heartbroken for opening himself up to a woman he barely knew. He was disgusted at himself for being so careless with his heart.

Promises To Keep

And she did it so effortlessly, Derrick thought as he drove home. He had a mind to go over to her apartment and ask her face to face, assuming she was there, why the charade. But deep down he knew the way he felt, he may have acted out of character, and felt it best to not be in her presence.

Derrick had to pass the high-rise building that housed Jacob West and Co. on his commute home. Although he'd seen the website listing of staff accountants who were employed by the company currently, and was sure that the information Monica had given him was correct, he still could not accept that Destiny would just flat out lie to him. Or maybe, he wasn't willing to accept he was so gullible for a pretty face. In either case, he'd made up his mind that he was going to stop in and ask a couple of questions.

After speaking with the information desk clerk, the human resources representative, and a few accountants entering and exiting the building, Derrick had no choice but to face the facts that he was played, big time. No one there had ever heard the name of Destiny Turner nor could they recognize the description Derrick gave of her.

"Listen sweetie, I've been here about 14 years. I've seen all types of women come through here, and believe me, it ain't too many with that much melanin if you get what I mean. So if anyone like that had ever worked here, I would have known," one of the accountants he'd met in the lobby coming back from lunch told him.

He walked into his apartment feeling drained and defeated. He opened his cabinet and grabbed the biggest rocks glass he could find. He filled it to the top with Crown Royal and before he could indulge, he heard a knock at the door. He wasn't expecting anyone, but there was only one person who could get through the gate and enter his building without being buzzed in. He hurried to hide his bothered demeanor, as to not let on to Monica how troubled he really was.

Opening the door brought on an unexpected surprise, as Monica pounced on Derrick like a lioness attacking her prey. She shoved Derrick against the wall behind his front door and immediately began to unbutton and unzip his pants. Monica was too much a lady to ever get on her knees, but she had a mean squat. She pulled Derrick's boxers down just low enough for her to position his staff directly in front of her.

Gradually she covered his bulging erection with the moisture of her mouth. Up and down, up and down, her oral movements saturated his shaft. Inch by inch, she devoured his package, until her face was pressed firmly against his pelvis.

Monica's deep throating ability was unmatched. She could make a man lose his shit without using her hands, and she was well versed at sucking off Derrick to the point of no return. She wasn't trying to please him or even make him feel better. She was sending a message. A message Derrick very well understood.

He stood there incapable of moving, enjoying the oral satisfaction Monica was providing. All this time he'd been so preoccupied with Destiny, that he'd mentally and physically forgotten the one woman who really loved him, flaws and all. Monica knew his upbringing. She'd been with him through high school and college. She was his rock in law school. She fought for him and with him inside and outside the courtroom. And in the blink of an eye, he denied her a chance at having real love in return because he was too selfish to give his all to her the way she'd given herself to him over the years.

Coming to this realization weakened him but also aroused him further in a strange way. Watching Monica's mohawk sway with the twist of her head as she went to town on his wood reminded Derrick of why she was once the most beautiful and loving woman in the world to him.

As Monica increased her rhythm, touching his chode in just the right place, Derrick could no longer hold on to the built up tension he acquired over the day. Monica could feel him becoming unsteady. Clinging on to the back of his legs, she sucked harder and harder, alternating her head to his shivers. Derrick could no longer withstand the clinic that Monica was putting on with her head game and tapped Monica's shoulder to alert her he was on the brink of explosion, but Monica ignored his warnings. He erupted right in the back of Monica's throat.

She didn't attempt to move.

Monica wanted to swallow every drop of Derrick and wanted him to know she was still willing to do anything and everything for him. She rose from her position and stared right into Derrick's eyes.

"Feel better?" she questioned with a sense of accomplishment in her voice. She knew what she had done and was quite proud of her ability to make a dick her bitch.

"Much better," Derrick confirmed. "I was just about to have drink. Shall I pour one for you?"

"Sweet offer, but nope. I have to go back to the office and finish up a few things, but I knew your mood and that you would need a pick me up after the disappointment at MEA. I came by to do my part in hopes you'd find that beautiful smile," Monica complimented.

"Thanks Mo... you did that and some. I'd expect you to allow me to return the favor later, say after dinner?" Derrick offered.

"It's a date. Now if you'll excuse me. And my toothbrush better still be in that bathroom," Monica said smirking at Derrick and heading in the direction of the bathroom to freshen up. He figured a final nightcap with Monica would be just what he needed to get thoughts of Destiny out of his head.

Remembering his drink that was on the counter, he reached for it and noticed he had a notification on his phone sitting next to it. It was an email from Bernice. He turned to see if Monica had returned and could still hear the running water from the bathroom sink. Derrick curiously opened the email with the subject line, *You're Gonna Want to See This.*

Upon opening the email, Derrick found a picture taken from the State of Connecticut Superior Court several years prior with an article attached. Glancing over the picture, he noticed the name in the caption was Devon Turner. The headline of the article read, "Hartford County Man Found

Guilty of First Degree Manslaughter Is Sentenced to 15 Years in Federal Prison." He was intrigued and began to open the article when Monica came in from behind and startled him.

"Hey! I'm heading out. But I'll be back, say 7:00?"

"Yeah ... 7 is good," Derrick acknowledged. Monica kissed him goodbye and headed out the door. Derrick locked the door behind Monica and continued to peruse the email from Bernice. Derrick noticed a familiar face in the picture, standing just to the right of the defendant - Destiny. It clicked. *This kid must be related to her. A brother perhaps?* And sure enough as he read the story attached, he was proven to be correct. He didn't understand what that had to do with her lying to him. He needed to call Bernice for clarification, but he didn't have to. Bernice was calling him.

"I was literally about to hit you up. This email? I don't get it. What's the connection with Devon and what does that have to do with Destiny not showing up today?"

"Derrick... Destiny didn't stand you up. She was kidnapped!"

"What!" Derrick yelled instantly rising to his feet.

"Derrick, I don't have much time cause I ain't even supposed to be in here, but the security guy got a little crush on me, so he let me slide with a bunch of shit. In any case, these side cameras from the parking lot were supposed to be broken. I was actually putting in a UAA request to have them fixed. Nobody was looking at these cameras and I only noticed because I needed the deck

154

numbers for the UAA request and saw the tape was rolling on something.

"Now from what I gathered, Devon got mixed up with some fucked up people. The guy they say he killed is the nephew of one of the biggest dope dealers in Boston. What if they kidnapped Destiny as payback?"

"Bernie, I need those tapes. I have to see for myself. Find a way to get a copy of those surveillances and call me back ASAP," Derrick demanded.

"Derrick, I cannot get access to the tapes outside of this booth. I don't have that kind of clearance."

"WELL FIND SOMEONE WHO DOES! I need to know what's going on!"

"Hey! Watch who the fuck you're yelling at! I'm doing my best to do you a favor. I don't give a fuck what happens to the bitch, you're the one in love with her and as good as the dick is, it ain't THAT damn good. Pull yourself together Derrick," Bernice fired back.

Bernice had never popped off on him that way before and it was well deserved. He crossed a line and raised his voice to one of the few people who knew the whole truth about this entire situation. The last thing he needed was for Bernice to be upset with him. She was the best assistant he'd ever had, and was damn good in bed. She'd been his accomplice in this plan the whole way and he was grateful. If all that fell through today, he'd still want a friendship with her.

He apologized instantly for the disrespect, "You're right Bernie. I apologize and thank you. Thank you for being you. Just please let me know what you find."

"I'll see what intel I can gather before I have to leave for the day. Just sit tight and wait for my call."

13
Not Who You Think I Am

It was thirty minutes to seven. Derrick had been pacing back and forth in his living room for the last three hours waiting for Bernice to call him back. The amount of patience it had taken to not blow her phone up was unbearable. Something had to be unveiled at this point. But he didn't want to make the mistake of pissing Bernice off again, so he waited as requested.

Time continued to pass him by and soon, he could hear Monica's heels strutting down the hallway outside. He unlocked the door so she wouldn't have to knock upon arrival and to Monica's dismay, Derrick looked exactly the same as he did when she left earlier.

"Derrick… what's up baby? You're not dressed?"

"Ummm... yeah about tonight Mo. I think I'm going to need a rain check."

Monica didn't hide her disappointment. "Wow Derrick. I was really looking forward to this. It's been a while since you and I had any real alone time. Now you told me that you were going to try. This doesn't seem like trying."

"Mo... Please don't do this right now. "

"Do what? Call you out on your bullshit."

"I'm just not as over today as I thought I was, and I just don't really feel like being out and about. I'm sorry. Another time. Please, just give me this."

"I've been giving you THIRTEEN FUCKING YEARS DERRICK! I have nothing left to give. For once in your life can you give to me?"

Derrick wished so badly he could fulfill the desire Monica craved, but he couldn't. He couldn't concentrate on Monica knowing that someone out there was holding Destiny hostage with no leads on who did it nor any means to help. He didn't have the ability to fake it anymore today. He frowned at Monica and dropped his head. Monica was infuriated.

"This isn't about today. It's not about losing lead counsel on the West case. You're upset over that girl from the bar."

"What? Monica... no, now you're reaching."

"Am I? You think I'm a fucking moron. Like I don't know this client of yours, this Destiny girl you were helping, is the same girl I caught you with at the bar. If you think I wasn't going to figure it out Derrick, then obviously you're not as bright of an attorney as I thought you were."

Before Derrick could rebut Monica, his phone vibrated. It was Bernice. He knew she would be calling about Destiny's whereabouts and had to answer the call, "Mo, I have to take this."

Monica looked to the ceiling and folded her arms in disbelief as Derrick turned and headed towards the kitchen to answer the phone:

"Bernie. Please tell me you got something good."

Bernice was breathing heavily in the phone and sounded as if she had tears in her eyes. Derrick could sense something wasn't right, "Bernice… what's wrong? Are you okay?"

"It was Monica!" Bernie yelled.

"Monica?" Derrick repeated.

"Monica kidnapped Destiny!" Bernice cried.

Derrick turned to face Monica when all of a sudden, it went black.

Promises To Keep

14
Abduction

7.5 Hours Earlier

Destiny gave herself one last look over in her rearview mirror. She slid the bobby pin on her hair to re-pin her bangs and touched up her lip-gloss with a slight hint of peach to match the natural toned makeup she donned and khaki colored dress she wore. Her legs glistened when she stepped out of her car and the sashay in her walk was far more defined than usual. She knew she was at MEA for business, but she was more than anything yearning to see Derrick.

Their weekend together had been amazing, and by the time it was over, she wholeheartedly knew that Derrick was the man for her. By the third time they'd made love, she had already determined in her mind that she was going to come clean about the whole thing. She considered that it may upset Derrick in the beginning, but concluded that the chemistry between them was strong enough to overcome this set back and start fresh. She wanted Derrick to know that the only reason she felt compelled to do this was because she wanted to help her brother. And she was still very committed to doing that. But Destiny would find another way. Another way that would allow her to be honest with Derrick and finally fly the straight and narrow.

As she approached the elevator in the parking garage, a random car flew through the garage ignoring the speed bumps and damn near ran into the gates. The car was speeding so rapidly, she almost lost her balance trying to move out of the way.

"Slow down asshole!" Destiny yelled at the driver. However, unbeknownst to her, she was not alone. Before she could spin around to take another step, an unidentified person placed a handkerchief across her face, putting her to sleep instantly.

...

The cold water smacked Destiny's face and she arose dazed and confused. Gradually coming to her senses, she panicked more and more as she assessed the seriousness of her situation. Her attempt to scream was hindered by the sock stuffed in her mouth and taped to her face, gagging her mouth shut. Her movements were limited to minor scoots, as she was bound to a chair by both legs and arms with multiple zip ties that were so tight, they were turning her wrists purple.

It was dark and hard for Destiny to pinpoint where she was exactly, but she could tell she had to be in some building that was under construction. There were boards in some places and building tools in others. She prayed to God those tools were for the creation of something, and not the destruction of her limbs.

Destiny had been frightened many times before. In the lifestyle she led, growing up homeless, and having to do whatever you could to survive, there were obviously times where she had been put in precarious circumstances. But, this was the first time she actually feared she was going to die. Tears fell down her face uncontrollably. She saw no scenarios in her head where this played out in her favor.

Shortly after her revelation, she heard voices.

Laughter.

A woman's laughter.

She knew who had her there. Whoever was doing this to her was highly amused.

Sick bitch she said in her head. The mystery chick that had ruined her life the last couple of months appeared from the shadows clapping.

"Bravo, my dear. Bravo," the woman applauded. "You did a great job of setting my traps for Derrick. But see there's just one little problem," the woman exclaimed as she stepped closer to Destiny.

"You my dear. You!" Her voice swiftly switched to a heinous tone. "You're so good, I almost believed you myself. That you would follow through with the plan to put an end to Derrick Goodwin as we know it. But then you decided to catch feelings. Then you further decided you wanted to come clean to Derrick. And to do what? Win his heart? Ha! I got news for you honey: he doesn't have one.

"Now I can't allow you to come foil my plan, can I? Of course not. That's a no go my dear. See, as good as you are with the charade of making people believe you're this victim in need of a good man and good lawyer to save you, that's how good I am at paying people to bug appliances, vehicles, and anything else I feel will give me a heads up on what my pawns are thinking when my plan is in motion. Tsk tsk tsk. You can't be trusted not to fuck it up. So, I had to intercept. Because you walking into that board room would have ruined everything. And I am so close to the finish line.

"Fortunately for me, this is turning out better than I originally planned. But unfortunately for you, this is where your contract is cancelled. "

Destiny's eyes widened larger than a full moon. The waterworks continued and you could hear Destiny pleading for her life through the gag. The more struggled to get free, the more she hurt herself in the process. The zip ties grew sharper around her wrists with each turn. They were beginning to pierce her skin, forming cuts that started to bleed.

Her capturer continued to snicker in enjoyment at Destiny's effort to escape, knowing full well she made it virtually impossible for her to do so.

"I'm going to let you have fun here. I've got some other people who I need to pay a little visit to. But you? Yeah, you'll be dead soon enough. No food. No water. Enclosed area, so your oxygen will run out soon. If you're lucky, you'll force a panic attack and croak sooner than later. Either way, you'll never see me again. You'll never see Derrick again. You'll never see anyone EVER again."

The woman 's voice echoed in the shadows as she disappeared the same way she came in, leaving Destiny alone to rot.

Promises To Keep

15
Arrested Development

BANG! BANG! BANG!

Derrick was in a state of bewilderment as to why he was on his kitchen floor and who in the hell was knocking on his door so hard. As he tried to stand, the knocks seemed to get louder and louder until finally he could hear what sounded like officers yelling through the door.

"YOU HAVE UNTIL THE COUNT OF 5 TO OPEN UP THE DOOR OR WE ARE COMING IN!" an officer yelled.

Derrick hurried to his feet but had no idea what the fuss was all about. He opened the door with the intention to find out why police officers were at his home and instead found himself in handcuffs with his Miranda rights being read to him:

"Mr. Derrick Goodwin?" the arresting officer asked to ensure he was detaining the correct person.

"Yes, I'm Derrick. What is going on?" Derrick asked trying to gain clarity.

"Mr. Goodwin, I have a warrant for your arrest for the double homicide of Rich McEnroe and Bernice Wright. You have the right to remain silent. Anything you say can and will be used against you in a court of law. You have the right to an attorney. If you cannot afford an attorney, one will be provided for you. Do you understand these rights?"

"Whoa... whoa! Are you kidding me? There's been some kind of mistake!" Derrick appealed to the officers. He couldn't believe what he was hearing. Rich was dead? And Bernice! This was wrong. This was all wrong.

"Mr. Goodwin do you understand these rights?" the officer asked once more, demanding a response.

"Yes, I'm an attorney, of course I understand these rights, but you guys have the wrong person. Please don't do this," Derrick begged. But it mattered not. He was cuffed and taken to the station for booking. Derrick knew this was going to be a long night.

...

"We can be all night Mr. Goodwin, but we have your fingerprints at the scene. We know you did it. We just want to know why?" Detective Martindale asked Derrick.

The two had been in there for what seemed liked hours, but it was only thirty minutes in reality. Derrick knew this officer well. He'd arrested some of Derrick's former clients, including St. James several years ago. With Derrick being a lawyer, Martindale knew the usual under the radar interrogation tactics wouldn't work. He had to be more conventional, more by the book… and he hated it. But nailing a lawyer for murder was something the department would have enjoyed and he certainly would have loved having that notch on his record. But Derrick was adamant on declaring his innocence.

"Come on MD. You know me. You know I didn't do this. How many times have I been here? This department doesn't have the best track record of getting it right. Don't let this be another one of those times."

Martindale sat the pictures of the two victims from the crime scene on the table. Derrick couldn't bare to see, especially not Bernice. His heart sank looking at her lying here. Bernice was bae. That was his girl. He cared for her, and to know that someone could slit her throat and leave her in a pool of blood in the bathroom was heartless. He turned his head away, as he felt the swell of tears in his eyes. And while he hated Rich, he never would have poisoned him. But Martindale didn't care.

"That girl was your assistant Goodwin. What could she possibly have done so horrendous that you felt the need to murder her in cold blood?"

Promises To Keep

"I DIDN'T FUCKING DO THIS TO HER!" Derrick shouted. He pushed the pictures from the table to the floor. His temper was getting the best of him and he knew any signs of anger would ultimately be used against him. It was a difficult task to remain calm when your life was literally flashing before you. Murder was a serious crime. Double murder was even more monstrous. But a double murder, committed by Derrick Goodwin, would make national news. He didn't know who was doing this to him or why, he had to get out of this and fast.

"Listen, I worked at McEnroe and Associates. My fingerprints are bound to be all over that place. That doesn't prove anything. Who can place me there? Where are your witnesses?"

"Exactly the same questions I have," said a voice from behind Martindale. Monica entered, swinging the door into the room open.

"Ms. Lawrence. How did I know?" sighed Detective Martindale.

"My client and I need a word. We'd prefer that conversation took place in the attorney conference room. And save me the bullshit MD. We know it exists and we have a right to speak confidentially."

Det. Martindale and Monica made eye contact and as he stood to exit, Monica added, "And don't you dare play me. You better take us in the correct conference room. You know what I mean by that," Monica stated hardheartedly.

She looked directly at Martindale who knew she meant business. Derrick knew not to say one thing to Monica

170

until they were in a safe space. The moment they entered the conference room and both were sure they could speak freely, Derrick let off.

"What the fuck is going on Monica? Seriously. Murder? I can't go down for a murder I didn't commit and you know I didn't commit this. "

"How do you know you didn't commit this?" Monica inquired.

"What do you mean? Maybe because I know I'm not capable of murder!"

"Your fingerprints were found on the murder weapon. That's going to be hard to disprove. By the way, where were you doing the time of the murders?"

"Are you seriously asking me this?"

Derrick was stunned at Monica's demeanor. She was treating him like a real criminal and someone seriously capable of killing his boss and his assistant. He didn't know what was worse: asking him where he was or the fact that he couldn't remember where he was.

Derrick sat down in the chair and put his head in his hands. He genuinely couldn't remember his whereabouts. "All I remember is waking up and having the cops banging on my door. I can't remember the hours before that. I genuinely don't know. But I know me. So do you Mo. You know I didn't do this."

"This is what I know: you have a dead employer who many know you have a tumultuous relationship with, who also happened to embarrass you earlier in the day when he didn't give you lead counsel on a case. He turns up dead, and your fingerprints are on the murder weapon, but you

171

have no alibi. Moments later your assistant is also found dead and again, your fingerprints on the knife with no alibi. That's what I know. That's what they know." Monica gathered, pointing to the door where the cops were standing outside.

It was at that moment that Derrick realized how hot the shit he was in really was. Why couldn't he remember past waking up on the floor? Who was doing this to him? Who wanted to ruin him? So many unanswered questions. But first things first, he had to officially hire Monica as his attorney.

"Okay, there has to be holes in this story. There's a real killer out there and we need to figure out who would want to ruin me enough to make this happen. But I need to officially declare you my attorney so we can get to work and you can get me out of here. So, you're hired. Now, we need to get the judge to grant me bail. I know that's a tall task for a murder suspect, but with my record and reputation, should be easier than others. Also…"

"Hold on partner," Monica interrupted, "who says I want to be your attorney?" Derrick turned to her puzzled.

"Who else Mo? You're the best out there. And you're my girl."

"Oh, I'm your girl now. Well, I guess that creates a conflict of interest."

"Mo…what are you doing? Seriously." Derrick questioned Monica sincerely.

"As a friend, I came down here as your acting attorney. But those are all the favors I have left unless you can tell me you're through with Destiny."

"Monica. I don't have time for this. My life is on the line and you're seriously bringing up Destiny? She's just a client, my God!"

"You're a fucking liar Derrick," Monica uttered. "Even with your life on the line, you still can't be honest. What's it going to take for you to see she's worthless just like Devon and never going to be good enough for you?"

Devon? Hearing that name was like a bullet hitting Derrick in the back of the head. Suddenly, his mind started seeing an article from Bernice, a picture of Devon and Destiny, a phone call about Destiny being kidnapped and … Monica. Bernice warned him about Monica. It was all coming back to him now. He didn't think it would be wise to let on that he knew, but it was becoming clear to him why Monica was so concerned about Destiny.

Derrick snapped back into the moment, and this time he altered his approach to cater to Monica's insecurities.

"Monica. You're right. I was kind of feeling Destiny. But she's no you. She'll never be you. Look at us right now. No one has ever had my back like you. No one ever will. I'm not lying when I say it's over for Destiny."

"Swear it."

"You have my word Mo."

Monica focused on Derrick, waiting to see any signs that would disclose he was playing her. But once she was satisfied with this elation of love for her, she knocked on the door to alert the guard their conversation was over.

Promises To Keep

"Give me one hour," she told Derrick.

16
Lost & Found

A woman of her word, Monica was able to have a judge grant bail for Derrick within the hour. Felony charges were tough and murder suspects were almost always denied bail, but due to Derrick's reputation, he was considered a low flight risk and somehow was given the ability to go free until his arraignment. Money was a distant issue for Derrick, so paying the $250,000 amount was the least of his worries. He also had to relinquish his passports, but that was also a small price to pay for his freedom and the opportunity to figure out who was trying to destroy him.

Upon his release, he naturally wanted to go to MEA.

"Are you crazy Derrick?" Monica expressed. "You get off on bail and the first place you want to go is back to the crime scene? That's not a good idea. I can't support that."

"Mo, you have to take me back to my office. I have to see Joe number one, and number two there are some items I have to get from my office," he rebutted.

Monica was very hesitant to agree. She didn't believe it was smart for Derrick to be at the very place he was being accused of murdering two people. She thoroughly advised him about not going to the office as his legal counsel. However, Derrick sensed it was more her resistance of wanting to go to MEA.

Once they pulled up to the front door, Derrick insisted that Monica wait in the car. He assured her that it would only take a moment to run up to his office and he would be back in 10 mins.

"I just want to get in, grab something from my desk, get out, and help clear my name," Derrick proclaimed.

Monica caved in. "You've got 10 minutes, and that's it."

"That's all I need babe," Derrick guaranteed.

Derrick headed into the building and rushed straight up to Joe. He found him in his office gazing out of the window miserably taking in the night sky. Joe was always there later than everyone else and why, no one ever knew. It was close to 11:00pm and nearly every office in the building was closed. But it made sense why Joe would, on this day, be around a little later than normal.

Derrick recognized all of this was certain to have an effect on Joe. He'd been at MEA since the beginning. Chris and Rich were like sons to him. So was Derrick. All of this happening at once had to feel like a mountain on his shoulder.

Derrick tapped the door lightly to grab Joe's attention.

"What in the hell are you doing here kid? There are cameras everywhere for the evening news. You shouldn't be here," Joe warned.

"Joe, I didn't kill anyone, you have to believe that," Derrick implored.

"Kid, I never presumed you did. But it's not what you know, it's what you can prove."

"Precisely why I need your help. I can't believe I'm saying this, but I think somehow Monica is involved. I can't pinpoint exactly how, but I know she's in trouble and may have gone in over her head. I blame myself for driving her near this edge, but I'm hoping she hasn't fallen off.

"She's been acting weird. Borderline psycho even. And earlier today, she hit me with something. Knocked me out cold. I woke up to the police knocking on my door telling me about Bernie and Rich and framing me as the suspect. She called herself being my attorney and 'helping' out, but the whole time she was there instead of focusing on why I was being setup and who could have done it, she was asking me about Destiny, who I also just found out is the sister of that dude who was charged with manslaughter for killing that out of town kid."

177

"Turner. Yeah. I remember that case. But wait, did Monica know that? That they were related? You know her firm handled that case," Joe enlightened.

Derrick stopped pacing Joe's office and shifted his attention directly to Joe. This perplexing situation just got a bit more complicated for Derrick.

"Joe, are you sure?"

"Well, I have a buddy over there. Let me call him and see what he can remember."

"Joe, I need that info ASAP. How soon can you talk to him? I need to run down to my office. Monica is who dropped me off and I told her ten minutes. The way her crazy has been set up lately, if I don't hurry back she'll come looking for me," Derrick said to Joe.

"Kid, go to your office. Keep your cell close. I'll call you as soon as I hear something."

Joe patted Derrick on the shoulder, reminding him that he still had allies and people supporting him. Derrick understood the gesture and silently nodded in gratitude.

By the time that Derrick arrived at his office, he could feel the ball welling up in the back of his throat. It was starting to really set in that Bernice was gone. Walking past her desk made it all too real. It sank in that he'd never smell that perfume he loved so much. He took a moment to reminisce on more than just their sexual encounters, but over the years how she'd been a true asset for him. She would be missed. He wiped his face of the tears that began to fall, and rubbed his fingers across her face on the picture that was still sitting on her desk. Seeing this office without her only motivated him more to find out who was behind her murder and why.

He opened his computer in his office just to see if Bernice had one last closing act in her. If those surveillance videos have been uploaded to his computer, he could at least get a better idea of what Bernice saw that lead to the conclusion that Monica was involved. It could also have linked what happened to Destiny, to the murder of Rich and Bernice. It was worth a try.

Derrick struck gold when he noticed a new file uploaded to his personal drive earlier that day.

"Bernice you are amazing girl," he whispered to himself. He didn't have time to look at the file, but had an external USB in his drawer that he could download the file to and take home to examine there.

Just then, his phone vibrated. It was Monica. He couldn't answer. He fully recognized ignoring her may not have been the best of ideas, but he could not allow her to come to his office. He couldn't risk having her walk in and finding the video footage. With only a few minutes left in the file transfer, Derrick's phone vibrated once more, only this time it was Joe.

"Perfect timing Joe," Derrick answered while grabbing the USB from the computer and walking out to lock his office door.

"We'll see about that. I just talked to my buddy who confirmed that not only was their office handling the case, but Monica was lead counsel. Rumor has it her case had holes. Should have been an easy walk, but instead kid got a conviction and is now doing a 15 year sentence. No one in the firm can understand how that case stuck."

Derrick stood at the elevator dumbfounded before hanging up the phone on Joe. Not only did Monica know Devon, she had represented him. So that means she knew Destiny too. Even when she saw her months ago at the bar, she had to know that was Destiny. This was going down an ugly path and Derrick wasn't emotionally equipped to handle the way this package was unraveling.

Lost in thoughts, he noticed he hadn't pushed the elevator button down but saw a neighboring elevator on the way up from G (Garage). That's Monica, Derrick assumed. He almost headed for the stairs, but backtracked once he remembered that would let him out right in the front of the news crews that were reporting live on the side of the building. Derrick called on Bernice once more and decided to go out from their own stomping ground: the North wing.

Practically running to safeguard from being seen by Monica getting off the elevator, he headed for the North Wing staircase. Eyeing the exit door, he carefully maneuvered himself through the construction taping only to hear something from the break room area. He wanted to ignore it. He was sure it was a mouse or something. But then he thought about Bernice. How she waited for him to find her in there and what became of their relationship after their random encounter. Maybe this was Bernice's spirit telling Derrick to just look through for old time's sake. But whatever that scratching sound was, it diverted his attention from the exit door. Against his better judgment for a second time, he elected to enter the room. And just like last time, he found the surprise of a lifetime.

Promises To Keep

17
The Wrong Girl

When Derrick saw Destiny he was relieved, shocked, and angered all at the same time. He hastily moved to aid her, first removing the gag from her mouth.

"Oh my God. Oh my God Derrick. I thought I was going to die. I thought I was going to die," Destiny cried out over and over.

"You're not going to die. I'm going to get you out of here. I promise you that."

Derrick stood up to look around the area to find a knife or something sharp enough to cut the zip ties off her hands. It was dark and warmer than usual. He was beginning to sweat, partially from the heat and partially

from the frustration of not finding any tools sharp enough
to free Destiny.

"Derrick, I have to tell you something," Destiny began.

"You can tell me anything and everything once you're
safe, but I have to get you out of here," Derrick interjected.
There had to be something sharp in a construction site and
no sooner after thinking it did he find mini pliers in a
toolbox. If they were sharp enough, they would do the
trick. He clipped and clipped a few times until finally he
was able to nip away and break the zip ties.

The two embraced. It felt damn good to hold her.

"Derrick, listen to me please," Destiny sobbed.

"I'm listening baby…I'm listening," Derrick comforted
as he wiped the tears from her eyes.

"I never worked for Jacob West," Destiny began, "and I
wasn't harassed. Someone made me make it all up. I don't
know who.

"At first I just wanted the money," she continued. "I
needed the money to get my brother out of jail. He didn't
do the things they say he did and I know that, so I knew
that the money would help with his appeal. They wanted
me to ruin you. They wanted me to push you as far as I
could and watch you burn. And I was gonna do it. I don't
know why, but I was. But that was before I knew you. And
then I saw them try to run you over with the car and I
knew I cared for you. I wanted to tell you in the park, but I
started receiving threatening messages about my life, and
your life, and Devon's life. I felt like I couldn't get out. But

I had to tell you because I love you. I couldn't continue with this lie and I couldn't continue to hurt you."

Destiny's sobs grew louder and louder. She leaned in to cry harder on Derrick's shoulder and he welcomed it, trying to console her. He didn't care about any of that. All that mattered was that she was safe, she was alive, and she was in his arms.

Those factors alone should have been enough to warrant a celebration for Derrick, but all they did was provide a temporary memory loss. The couple froze, looking up to find Monica standing next to them once they heard the sound of a gun cock. Derrick was so absorbed in the finding of Destiny that he'd forgotten Monica was on his trail. He was soon reminded with a 9mm pointed at the back of his head.

"Now I could have sworn you swore to me that this bitch was done. And once again, like a dummy, I believed you. You know Derrick, you are becoming a habitual liar."

"Monica, what are you doing? Put the gun down," Derrick pleaded.

The already dark, small area just seemed to get a bit smaller with a gun now on play and there were plenty of opportunities for things to go wrong in a construction zone. Monica adding a gun to the mix in a dimly lit location only made matters worse and more dangerous.

Derrick turned slightly, facing the barrel of the gun and Destiny lifted her eyes to find a face she'd seen before.

"I know her," Destiny said coming to a revelation. It had been years, but she now recognized Monica. "She was my brother's attorney. How did I not recognize you before? Wait a minute... Was it you? Were you the one behind this the whole time?"

Monica began to back away from Derrick, heading into the break room where the light was brighter and her face could be seen. That break room was once a place of solace for Derrick, where he could escape the pressure of the office, eat his lunch in peace, or just vibe with Bernice. Now it was potentially going to be his tomb. Everything was happening fast. He never saw this coming from Monica.

"Monica, no matter what you've done or didn't do, it doesn't matter. But right now, put the gun down and let's talk about this."

"There's nothing I want to say to you Derrick Goodwin. You're nothing like the man I thought you were. You're a coward. You're just like your father."

"Monica, I've made mistakes. Who hasn't? But this can be worked out. Come on Mo. Thirteen years. Don't do something you'll regret," Derrick said trying to sway Monica to drop her weapon. "But just like my father Mo? Come on. You don't really believe that do you?" Derrick asked.

Monica couldn't stop the tears that had begun to fall down the side of her face. She was trying so hard to be the tough girl that she had always been, that she always needed to be. But even in the most vulnerable state, she was unsure if she could actually hurt Derrick. She considered lowering the gun in her mind and her arms soon began to follow.

Derrick could sense he was getting to her. As he was preparing to keep the emotional clamp on Monica while she was contemplating her actions, he was silenced once he saw the woman in all black creep before the three of them. She stood next to Monica for several seconds observing the situation. She placed her hands on Monica's hand and raised the gun back up, pointed not at Derrick this time, but at Destiny. Monica cracked a freakish smile, as if she knew what was to happen next. The woman leisurely began to take off her hat and the customary durag she wore underneath.

"Who... who are you?" Derrick asked. The moment of truth was upon them. Destiny had been wondering for months, waiting for the person who had literally turned her life upside down to unveil him or herself. Derrick was frozen solid. Unable to move. Unable to breath. Unable to comprehend what he was watching unfold before his very eyes, he saw the perp that was calling all the shots. And so did Destiny.

"No fucking way... NO FUCKING WAY!" Derrick screamed.

Promises To Keep

18
Mommy Dearest

This has to be a joke, Derrick thought. There was no way the woman standing before them could be behind any of this.

"Monica you bitch! Why is my mother here? Why the fuck is my mother here?!" Derrick yelled.

"You watch your mouth!" Ruby shouted. "I didn't raise you to speak to women that way. Hell, I didn't raise you to do a lot of the shit you do. I don't even recognize you half the time."

"I don't recognize you right now," Derrick whispered confusingly. How could his mother be behind this? It wasn't in her nature. Derrick had always known his mother to be timid, reserved. She never stood up for herself. She wasn't the type to take matters into her own hands, or any matters for anything. She let people run over her and it was the one thing that Derrick hated most about his mom. She was too fearful to ever be the mastermind of a plot that would involve murder and deceit, let alone anything that would cause the destruction of her only son.

But what Derrick didn't account for was the hurt his mother had built up over the years. She was heartbroken; tired of the bullshit from men.

"This is me Derrick. The me that's been created by the countless sleepless nights, disrespect, and downright bullshit that your father has put me through for 30 years. He has taken everything from me: my dignity, my strength, my pride. I allowed your father to emotionally abuse me over and over again for the sake of you being raised in a two-parent household with parents who loved you. But, what I did not anticipate was you growing up to be in many ways worse than HIM."

As Monica kept the gun pointed at Destiny, Ruby continued walking closer to Derrick until she was right in his face. "You're a womanizer. You're following in his footsteps. You don't appreciate a good woman when you have one. You talk to me so cold, like I didn't change your diapers, boy. But I thought eventually, you would change. I thought to myself, 'my son will see the error of his ways and settle down.' I thought, 'my son will be better than bastard that conceived him.' And then came Monica. I always knew she was going to be the one for you, since you two were classmates. I've always loved her as the daughter I never had. But once again, you made a fool of me, son.

"You couldn't see what you had right in front of you. And for what, for women like her?" Ruby said angrily pointing at Destiny.

"So you tried to run me over Ma? You wanted to kill me?"

"Son, I never wanted you to die. Why would I kill my son?! But you needed to be taught a lesson. You need to be reminded how much you needed Monica. I thought maybe if you could see how much trouble this Destiny character really was, you'd choose Monica. That girl is a liar. She's trash. And when the police came knocking at your door, who was there to help you? To save you? Not her. It was Monica. I needed to break you so low that you had no choice but to go back to Monica. Which meant that all the people in the way needed to go. Rich would never let you be partner, which meant that you and Monica could never have your own firm. Bernice was just a piece of ass. She meant nothing to you. And besides, Monica never liked her as your assistant."

Derrick's eyes widened, "I can't believe I'm asking this, but did you... did you kill my boss and my assistant?"

Ruby glimpsed at Monica who shrugged her shoulders. Derrick stared at his mother in complete perplexity while awaiting an answer. It was like he didn't even know her. He glanced back at Destiny who was standing in front of the chair she was once tied to. She knew if she attempted to move that she would run the risk of either being shot or she'd trip and fall as it was dark in the small construction area. The two ceiling lights from the break room were only bright enough to see faces and shadows. But sudden movements could leave anyone injured. She stood there, shook that this whole idea of taking down Derrick stemmed from his own mother. She could see Derrick looking at her and she looked back, wanting so badly to reach for him. The look in Derrick's eyes assured her that they would be fine, but their eye contact did not go unnoticed by Monica. Fury took over her and Monica could no longer contain her temper.

"Even in my face, with a gun pointed to her head, you continue to disrespect me," Monica cried aloud. "Yes, I was the lawyer on your brother's case. I could have easily gotten him off that manslaughter charge too. The DNA didn't match. But I purposely didn't include the blood test results in the evidence file. I needed him to go jail. Sometimes moving up in the company means you have to get your hands a little dirty. Sending Devon to jail was favorable in the eyes of the district attorney's office, which is an office I will one day hold. So yes, that meant losing a case and unfortunately for you, it meant losing your brother. But there's a valuable lesson to be learned here. You see in the end, I ALWAYS win," Monica belted out nonchalantly.

"You did what!" Destiny lost it. She saw nothing. She heard nothing. She didn't care about anything. This woman just admitted to intentionally locking up her brother... her innocent brother.

I am going to fuck this bitch up, Destiny silently declared. "You BITCH!" Destiny screamed and without warning or notice, she lowered her head and ran directly at Monica, spearing her against the wall in the well-lit break room. Destiny was getting the better of Monica, who was caught off guard by the attack. Monica, still clinging to the gun, and Destiny, trying her hardest to take it from her, tussled leaving Derrick unsure of how to break the two apart with a live gun in play.

Somehow managing to stand to their feet, Destiny continued to attempt to rip the gun from Monica's hand.

"I'm going to kill you," Destiny shouted.

"Not today bitch," Monica retorted.

With both their hands on the gun and the barrel pointed straight up in the air, a loud firecracker sound rang through the breakroom twice, almost deafening to Derrick's ears. Two bullets pierced a hole in the ceiling, loosening the light fixture that came crashing down with a bang that frightened both Monica and Destiny. In an effort to miss being struck by the falling fixture, Monica relinquished her hold on the gun, causing her and Destiny to fall backwards and hit their heads on the ground.

Upon standing, Derrick found Destiny on the floor but conscious. Monica was on the other side of the room, but knocked out cold from the head blow to the floor. Destiny rose to run to get help but stopped abruptly staring into what appeared to be a pool of blood.

Promises To Keep

19
Promises

Mom! Derrick ran to the opposite side of Monica to find the fixture had fallen directly on his mother, knocking her onto the wooden planks that had not been taken into the construction area. Ruby's side had been penetrated by the broken florescent bulbs and the metal sidings of the ceiling lamp. She bled profusely with tears in her eyes as Derricked rushed to her side to help her. He knew he couldn't move her, it would increase what already appeared to be a loss of too much blood. He panicked. He couldn't stop the tears from falling. No matter what she had done, she was still his mother. The way the blood was oozing from her side, he needed to get her help and fast.

Destiny assessed the scene. Seeing that Monica was still comatose, she figured it was now or never to get help, or better yet, to leave.

Destiny knew this was her chance to run. As Derrick wept by his mother's side and Monica was out cold on the wall, this could be her chance to get away scot free away from everything. She still had the money. She heard Monica say her brother was innocent. She had everything she needed to run away and never return. Six months ago, she would have done just that. However, for the first time in her life, it wasn't just about her and her survival. She was in love with Derrick. Running away would mean running away from him. She didn't want that. She didn't want to lose him, even if that meant facing him in the aftermath for the part she played in it all.

The noise from the gunshots were loud enough for Joe, who was still in the building, to hear. Not many people knew that the north wing was still being accessed, not even Joe. He was quite surprised to run into Destiny coming from that direction, who led them to the whereabouts of Derrick and his mother in the North Wing break room. Within a matter of minutes, EMTs were on the scene, as well as law enforcement officers.

Monica gave a statement about what had transpired. She admitted she was jealous seeing Destiny and Derrick together. She recognized Destiny as the sister of her former client and confessed that she and Ruby conspired to ruin

Derrick's reputation as an attorney in an effort to teach him a lesson after she alerted Ruby of his infidelities.

"She snapped," Monica stated. "It was like she'd had enough and said to me we had to put a stop to Derrick before he could hurt me any further. She didn't want me to end up like her."

Monica told the police how she coerced Destiny to lie to Derrick in a setup to wreck his character at MEA. She knew that she mishandled Devon Turner's case and that she still held the evidence in her possession that could clear his name. She was sure Devon would be the key to keeping Destiny in line with the plan, even with little knowledge of what the plan's purpose actually was.

She disclosed she was driving the car that attacked Derrick and she had knocked him out cold in his apartment to take his fingerprints in order to plant them in Rich's office, as well as on the knife that killed Bernice. Monica swore she didn't commit the murders, and couldn't say for sure if Ruby was the culprit. All she knew was that once Derrick was facing murder charges, it was a no brainer that he was supposed to come running to back to her. She was stunned when that wasn't the case. She flipped… and so did Ruby.

Kidnapping Destiny was never a part of the plan, but the more Destiny caught feelings for Derrick, the more difficult it became to control her.

"We had to do something," Monica acknowledged. "If we didn't, she would have come clean right in front of everyone. So, I gave her chloroform in the parking garage to knock her out."

Promises To Keep

Monica's statement was able to clear Derrick's name of the murders and exonerate Destiny from any involvement.

Meanwhile, Derrick watched helplessly as the medical staff lifted his mother onto the gurney. The puncture wound was deep and the bleeding had not subsided. Ruby was slowly losing consciousness. The EMTs escorted her down the elevator to the ambulance, but the lifeline for Ruby was growing thin. She was barely breathing, holding on to Derrick the entire way. Something clicked in Derrick once the doors to the EMS were open. He couldn't muster the courage to step inside the ambulance. Ruby squinted at him as his hands began to slip away from hers.

"I'm so sorry momma," Derrick sobbed, whispering to her. "I know I drove you to do this and I'm so so sorry. But I have to know: Did you kill Rich and Bernice?"

Ruby rubbed the side of his face while grimacing in pain. He wept even more, feeling guilty and responsible for everything.

"I have to know Mom. I have to know," Derrick pleaded.

"Can you just be the man I raised you to be son? That's all," Ruby uttered faintly. "Just love her please. Just love her."

"I will Mom," Derrick promised, slowly releasing his hand from hers. She smiled, and tilted her head to the side. Her breathing slowed. Her heart rate dropped.

The EMT motioned for Derrick to hop inside and ride with them to the hospital, but Derrick shook his head no and backed away. "We're losing her! We're losing her!"

the EMT yelled as the door closed shut. Derrick watched the ambulance pull away, listening to the sound of the sirens speed off into the distance.

Promises To Keep

20
Epilogue

5 Years Later

"Your Honor. Ladies and gentleman of the jury. I think it's quite clear that my client had been falsely accused and the evidence against him is circumstantial. There is nothing that the prosecution has been able to present that fully places my client at the scene when the crime was committed. I hope you, being the smart men and women you are, realize this ploy to destroy a good man's name and find the right verdict. Plain and simple. The defense rests."

Derrick took his place next to his client as he finished his closing arguments. This was his third trial since opening D&D Associates. Nothing felt as good as representing your own name, your own clientele, and having a winning record to precede you.

He owed this small sense of happiness to Joe and Chris. They took over McEnroe & Associates after everything had gone down and finally cut him loose. Chris was kind enough to vouch for Derrick at this hearing with the ABA, testifying that he'd fulfilled all his obligations to be released from his probation. It felt good not to be under the clutches of someone micromanaging his day to day.

Derrick was happy, but it took a while to get there. Monica's trial was a hectic one. There were still so many unanswered questions, but Monica was going to have a long time to think about it following her 13-year sentence for assault, kidnapping, and accessory to a felony.

There was still no resolve as to who actually killed Rich and Bernice. This weighed on Derrick daily. He even sought out the help of a therapist. It bothered him that his family in some way played a role in the death of Bernice and he still had troubling coming to grips that it wasn't his fault. He burned a candle every night in her honor. It was yellow, and it smelled like a Caribbean breeze, just like Bernice.

The trial Derrick was working had been all over the news regionally. It was a massive case that had political implications. Everyone was tuned in to see the verdict, including the staff at the June Foxx Psychiatric Facility.

"Turn that up," one of the patients requested.

"Now you know that you aren't supposed to be watching this," the nurse responded.

"I know, I know. But that's my son... "

The nurse sighed, "Alright Ms. Ruby, just this one time. Don't make it habit."

Ruby sat there staring at the screen with the biggest grin on her face. She was ecstatic that her son was living his life and felt a sense of pride that she played a part in turning him on the straight and narrow. Ruby had narrowly survived her injury and after a psych evaluation was found unfit to stand trial. She had officially, in the eyes of the courts, lost her mind. But Ruby wasn't as crazy as people wanted to believe.

She smiled from ear to ear when she heard the foreman read the verdict of not guilty.

"He won!!! My son won!" Ruby exclaimed. The nurse on duty smiled back at Ruby, genuinely happy for the proud moment that Ruby was basking in.

After the verdict was read, Derrick made his way to the line of reporters who were waiting to hear his post-trial thoughts.

"Shhhh everyone. My son's talking on the TV," Ruby hushed to everyone. The nurse increased the volume so Derrick could be heard in the room by all.

"Well, it was a grueling case. But, I'm very pleased to be on the right side, the winning side of the law. I spent countless days and nights working on this that I neglected many things in my life, so as delighted as I am that my client will get his life back, I'm equally as happy that I can get back to my 2-year-old son and my fiancé."

Ruby's smile grew even larger, bragging loudly on Derrick's achievement. "Oh, my son has a son! And he's getting married!"

She knew she would never get to see her grandson in person. Derrick never came to visit, write, or anything. But she looked at that screen, content that he kept his word to her. She looked on as Derrick picked up this handsome caramel child who came running through the crowd, and she waited to see Monica's face as he leaned over to kiss a woman who was standing beside him.

Ruby's whole demeanor shifted. Her laughs turned to loud yells of rage. She grabbed her hair and began to yell at the TV. "NO… NO… NO!!!! NOT HER… NOT HER!!" She continued to shout and fuss. The nurses tried to control her, but to no avail. Orderlies were called to sedate her as she continued to scream at the screen. Finally, a staff member grabbed the remote to shut the television off right as the name Destiny Turner, Goodwin's fiancé appeared on the screen.

Nicki Charest

Sneak Peek

A Twisted Love II: Trapped In Paradise

The rain was coming down harder and harder. It was pitch black that night and the only thing that could be seen was the lights from the front of the plane and the reflectors on the runway. The noise from the aircraft engines was deafening, yet it mirrored mere silence compared the sound of Kash's heart beating out of her chest. Pounding with every breath she took, Kash was nervous and scared.

"Baby... you know me. You don't have to do this. I am begging you please, please don't do this. You are the only man I've ever loved, I swear it. You have to believe me."

Syncere looked in Kash's eyes, keeping the loaded Beretta M9 pointed in her direction, while watching the tears fall as she mercifully pleaded for her life. He wanted so badly to believe her words were genuine, but too much had happened at this point for him to trust her, no matter how much he loved her.

"I gave you every thing," Syncere shouted. "I let you in. I opened myself up to you. I told you things I've never shared with anyone. What the fuck Kash?"

"Syn, I swear to you, it wasn't me," Kash said sobbing uncontrollably.

"Then why are we here Kash? Huh? Why are you here with him?"

Alex lay unconscious on the ground. Syncere felt like a fool. Kash and Alex had played him, and he was hurt. There was nothing more in this world that Syncere hated like he did betrayal. And in this moment, his rage at the thought of being betrayed by Kash was more than his mind and heart could handle. He was out for blood.

"This was the plan all along, huh? To take me out? To take everything from me? To make me fall for you? Why would you do this Kash?"

Syncere was done letting his emotions get the best of him. He knew what needed to be done, even if he didn't want to do it, and it was time to tie up all loose ends. He took the safety off the Beretta and loaded the chamber.

Kash knew it was a wrap. She knew Syncere well enough to know that the moment she heard that gun cock, the decision to take her out had been made. She didn't know how to convince Syncere she was innocent of the one thing he despised more than anything when all the signs pointed to her guilt.

As she walked closer to Syncere, she placed her head right at the barrel of the gun. She had no answer for him and couldn't explain why they were in the situation they were in. She could only hope that his love for her would overpower his anger, and that Syn would come to his senses.

The two of them stood in the middle of Thomas Jefferson Airfield with a Gulfstream g650 private jet in their background. They gazed at each for one final moment before Syncere placed his finger on the trigger. Before he could fire the shot, Alex rose of out nowhere to tackle him from behind, dropping Syncere to the ground.

With the gun out of her face, Kash let out a sigh, having been holding her breath through the entire encounter, especially under the barrel of the gun. For a split second, she cried and grasped for air, but not for long. After taking a couple of seconds to collect herself, she stood up, and without thinking she jumped in between Syncere and Alex to break up the fight.

Tussling with the gun, Alex took his left hand and punched Syncere in the nose and in the stomach. The impact of the hit loosened Syncere's fingers, allowing Alex to knock the gun out of his hand and right at Kash's feet.

The water from the rain was starting to fall heavily in her eyes, but she could see that Alex was starting to stand and knew this was the only chance she would have to getting out of this alive. Kash looked at the gun, knowing she should have picked it up, but she couldn't. She instead looked at the plane ready for take off behind her. Someone was getting on that plane and Kash needed it to be her. She backed away from the gun and ran towards the airstairs.

"Kash NO!" Alex shouted while Kash ran. Hearing her name made her run faster, until suddenly a gunshot stopped her dead in her tracks and Kash dropped to her knees...

COMING WINTER 2019

About The Author

Nicki Charest is an author, writer, and poet from Detroit, MI. She holds a Masters of Arts in Multimedia Journalism and serves as digital audio producer for the sports conglomerate ESPN. Fascinated with telling mature stories at an early age, Nicki had over 50 poems, 15 songs, and several short stories written by the age of 13. She's performed at various open mic competitions and poetry slams around the city of Detroit and Raleigh, NC., including sharing the stage with renowned spoken word artist Dasan Ahanu. Now a married stepmother of one, Nicki is ready to share her stories with the world. Her first novel, *A Twisted Love*, was an Amazon Best-Seller and charted at No. 5 on the African American Erotica list. *Promises to Keep* is the second novel by the author in the erotic/thriller genre.

Connect With Nicki Charest

Website: www.authornickicharest.com
Facebook: Author Nicki Charest
Instagram: @NickiCharest
Twitter: @NickiCharest

UPCOMING NOVEL:
A Twisted Love II: Lost In Paradise (Coming Winter 2019)